Praise for Peter Handke
and *The Weight of the World*

"Time's impression on the world is Handke's reality . . . He sees clearly, reading the world with the care of a master novelist."
— Jerome Klinkowitz, *Chicago Tribune*

"**One of the most original and provocative of contemporary writers.**"—*The New York Times Book Review*

"Peter Handke must be acknowledged as one of the major voices in contemporary fiction today."—*Partisan Review*

"If Ann Beattie has become America's premier observer of disaffected 1960s radicals, Handke has taken as his fictional territory a similar generation of discontented Europeans—individuals who can be characterized above all by their passivity, their intellectual frustration and their inability to take part in meaningful interaction with others."
— *San Francisco Chronicle*

"In power and vision and range, Peter Handke is **the most important new writer on the international scene since Beckett.**"
— Stanley Kaufmann, *Saturday Review*

"Peter Handke was and is one of the most eminent narrative and dramatic writers of postwar Europe."—*Boston Globe*

"His prose is reminiscent of the writings of Henry James . . . a passion for understanding, for grasping the tortured complexities of contemporary life."—*The Philadelphia Inquirer*

"**Every word Peter Handke speaks has consequences.**"
— *The New Republic*

Works by Peter Handke available from Collier Books

Across

Slow Homecoming

Repetition

3 X Handke

2 X Handke

PETER HANDKE

The Weight of the World

Translated by Ralph Manheim

Collier Books

Macmillan Publishing Company

New York

Published by arrangement with Farrar, Straus and Giroux, Inc.

Collier Books
Macmillan Publishing Company
866 Third Avenue, New York, N.Y. 10022
Collier Macmillan Canada, Inc.

Library of Congress Cataloging-in-Publication Data
Handke, Peter.
    [Gewicht der Welt. English]
    The weight of the world / Peter Handke ; translated by Ralph
Manheim. — 1st Collier Books ed.
      p. cm.
    Translation of: Das Gewicht der Welt.
    ISBN 0-02-051490-5
    I Title.
PT2668.A5G413   1990
838'.91403—dec20
[B]   89-25242   CIP

Macmillan books are available at special discounts for bulk purchases for sales promotions, premiums, fund-raising, or educational use. For details, contact:

Special Sales Director
Macmillan Publishing Company
866 Third Avenue
New York, N.Y. 10022

First Collier Books Edition 1990

10 9 8 7 6 5 4 3 2 1

Printed in the United States of America

To whom it may concern

*Author and translator have
collaborated closely in preparing*
The Weight of the World, *and agreed to
delete certain passages, amounting to
about ten pages in all. Some of these—
fragmentary attempts to formulate a
political attitude—no longer struck the
author as compatible with the spirit of
the book. Other phrases or sentences
have been cut because their point
seemed inseparable from the German
language, and still others because,
on rereading them, the author
didn't like them any more.*

P.H. / R.M.

The Weight of the World

1 9 7 5

November

Sometimes I feel as if I had to stoop to go on living (the ultimate in resignation: "Never again will I have anything repaired")

He throws one leg over the other—they are forcibly untwined; he props up his elbows—they are pushed away; he puts his hands in his pockets—they are pulled out; he puts his hands in front of his face—they are wrenched away (intervene as soon as anyone touches himself)

Flight and pursuit: a woman is chasing a man. The pursuing woman tears off her wig and turns out to be a man; the fleeing man loses his hat and turns out to be a woman; they fall into each other's arms

Some policemen are blocking the way, but pretending not to know it; they stare straight ahead, but if anyone approaches, they frighten him away by tapping their gun holsters

A couple. The woman keeps going off to telephone; each time she comes back, she moves a little farther away from the man; but after her last phone call she throws her arms around him and so they remain

A man sits slumped in his chair; he tries over and over again to straighten up and look dignified, but keeps slumping down again; in the end he's content to stay that way

Dream sounds: "as if the house were full of thawing June bugs"

A man lays his hand on a woman's shoulder; the woman tosses back her hair and lifts her chin; the man puts his other hand on the woman's hip; at this point she slowly lowers her head until her hair covers her face entirely, breaks away from the man, moves about, goes forward, goes backward with her face curtained in hair, until it's impossible to tell where her face is and where the back of her head; a child comes along and looks for the woman's face

They fondle and despise each other at the same time

I lose patience with someone—because I'm not following his movements

Someone, in touching someone else, shows the facial expression of a person inspecting his fingertip after dipping it in a pile of dust

Imagine a long monologue consisting entirely of movements and actions; someone would enter stealthily and look on. The first person (whose actions have not been at all significant) would somehow feel caught and take fright

A person sees something that is hidden from us. Suddenly this person launches into a long sequence of silent gestures connoting horror and the approach of death. But we see only the person and not what the person sees

A woman doing the housework and drying her tears—both at the same time

Big fight; suddenly water starts flowing from a flowerpot over the heads of the combatants; they stop fighting and become absorbed in the flowing stream

One man walks back and forth in front of another; at last the second man looks up; then the first nods a silent goodbye and goes away

Agreed that no one can be forced to speak lying down. "Stand up! Speak!"

What makes me awkward: indifference (the listlessness that makes for slapstick)

He writes something in the air; the others look on expectantly and smile when he has finally finished

"I was no longer superficial—I had stopped thinking"

A man who just stands around with a ball-point pen in his mouth, senselessly putting things back in their place. The owner of a restaurant? No, the manager; in standing around, he holds on to the doorframe over his head with one finger or cleans his immaculate fingernails

Involuntarily, with a look of disgust, I beat time to the march music with my foot

Suppose I weren't allowed the gestures people make when they don't know what else to do: clicking the buckle of my wrist-watch strap, unbuttoning and rebuttoning my shirt, running my hands through my hair. In the end I'd have nothing to sustain me, I'd be lost

Covert pinching by one too cowardly to strike

That by now automatic look of disapproval when, for instance, I hear the roar of a motorcycle, when I'm jostled by someone running past, etc.

Getting even with Creation: the desire to sing out of tune at the top of my lungs

A woman striding vigorously, eyes straight ahead, stretches out a hand into the void for the child stumbling along after her

Someone drops something. The people at the next table look around, but only for a second

No luggage, nothing to carry; the joy of having your hands free: "Just a toothbrush"

A woman alone in the street, waiting for someone I can't see and smiling in his direction. Her strange movements in front of the shop window, her dance of expectancy, the way she clutches at her hair and looks up, the way she keeps turning to look at herself in the shop window. And then at last the man she has been waiting for appears, and the two of them leave quickly, without touching, without a word

Walking through the roar of the city. Wherever you go, someone's lying there hurt, with onlookers all around him and someone who has had a narrow escape explaining how it happened. And there's always a policeman on the spot, who says: *"C'est fini! Partez!"* —But even so, the structure is falling apart

The torch singer's tongue quivers in his mouth; he shuts his eyes in singing; his hand outstretched as though to reassure us; his painful frown as he sings; the way he shakes his hair; the way he woos the audience by holding one shoulder higher than the other; the way he topples with exhaustion in taking his bow; that "tired but happy" smile—as though, at least for a few minutes, he were showing people what yearning is and at the same time relieving them of theirs

In performing solemn actions (e.g., genuflecting in church), she would stick out her tongue in embarrassment

After the dance, when movements break off, and nothing remains but sounds of people leaving: "Appeasement moved into his heart"

In the crowd, a woman is pushing a man ahead of her, as men often do to women

Someone repeats an act of violence, because it made such a pleasant sound the first time

Under his dinner jacket a man is wearing a T-shirt with the inscription: *Faded Glory*

He uses his absentmindedness as a defensive weapon

In the sickroom: all afternoon, tulip petals fell to the floor

Trying to take a ball-point pen out of his pocket. What turns up first: coins, photos, toilet paper

Often, face and all, I belong to the crowd; but in the worst sense

He exhales so emphatically to show that he's bored

A lady paying: pointing her delicate fingers, she reaches into her purse and puts down the coin. After this unpleasant gesture (showing how she feels about money!), she smooths out her silk shawl

I walk around the city for hours, holding some object (a key, a piece of wood) and scraping it along fences, walls, housefronts; it's something I need to do; a great privation if it were forbidden!

I'm standing by the photo machine, waiting for pictures; a picture with a different face comes out—this could be the beginning of a story

"Yes, I feel dejected now, I feel the indifference between us— but I don't accept it any more!" (I used to accept indifference as a law)

A fine thing: suddenly to forget about one's history, one's past, to stop feeling that one's present happiness is endangered by what one used to be, as a child, an adolescent, etc.

They call her "standoffish"; but it's only that she doesn't take any relationship for granted

Once I realize the absurdity of my actions, I feel better

Already out in the street, I catch myself humming the jingle of the department store commercial (why not become a composer of jingles?)

Complete sense of failure; stop talking altogether

The girl's story: "I followed a man in the Métro. From station to station I felt more beautiful—when he finally spoke to me I was unapproachable; too beautiful"

"When you're with me, I can't help crying harder." — "Why?" — "Because when I hurt myself I see you, and then I want you"

Passing a darkened window behind which a friend used to live

Days full of life and meaning, quiet wintry feeling in the railroad stations; and then days when you keep biting the same place on your lip

Two people lie side by side in two bathtubs, talking like two people who have just endured great hardships in a Western

The man switches on the car radio and the woman asks: "Do you expect music to save you again?"

An old man sat resting in a half-flooded lime pit, up to his neck in lime water; that was his usual resting place

A child is singing a song; it has been told to *say* the words, but it can't

"What your parents were, what your parents did—cut it out, I'm sick of it!"

A woman who thinks her sex organs are ugly

He stared at me as though to imprint my features on his mind and denounce me later on

To look up at the sky and the drifting clouds and think: No, I will never commit suicide!

Covered with fallen leaves in the twilight, the square suddenly begins to look like a park. A feeling of happiness that I might have at any time

The saleswoman in the department store—as if she hadn't expected a kindness in a long while, not from anyone

At the sight of the fallen leaves: the thought that in another year there may be nothing more to discover

Before taking her packages into the house, the woman stops on the sidewalk and waits for something, for a short-term solution

"I must stop feeling guilty over feeling nothing"

Look at myself now and then, it helps me to think (ruin my eyes by staring at myself)

When I talk about myself, it's often out of sheer embarrassment

Trying to forget the thoughts or images I've already had, so as to avoid repeating them and clinging to them, while emptiness spreads *between* them

Sometimes I feel as if I ought to pull my mouth apart with my fingers, to keep from being the same person

"What you've told me about myself—naturally I tell myself the same thing, but maybe it's good to hear it from someone else, because there are times when I don't believe myself"

My way of thinking is often so wrong, so untenable, because I think as if I were talking to someone else

I once knew someone who was so much in love with his thoughts that they brought tears to his eyes

That woman was walking so elegantly, and now, all of a' sudden her gait is slovenly, lewd, and vulgar; she's visibly relieved

Drop everything; then fall to the floor (dropping whatever you're holding, one thing at a time—then take a deep breath)

A woman sitting by herself; she slips off her shoe and, when someone approaches, slips it on again

After he has looked at her a long time and she has kept evading his eyes, ignoring him, she suddenly smiles and returns his gaze; disappointed, cheated, he strikes her without thinking

A gentleman wants to be alone. (Already there's no one else in the room.) He rings for his servant and says in response to the knock: "Don't come in!" At last he is alone

The man on the stretcher in the back of the ambulance: fear of death gives him a look of candor

A beautiful, serious-looking woman. Suddenly her frozen face bursts into a smile—it's as if she were making water

I'm satisfied with myself when I have managed to be laconic

She sees a movie about a woman, made by a man, and thinks: Who does he think he is?

He sits up straight and starts staring into space. The woman: "Now don't start thinking again, not in front of me!"

Sometimes, after seeing a movie or reading a book, I feel so serious that I decide to get along with everyone; but when I start meeting people and talking, I make the same old grimaces

A beautiful, awkward woman (a character for a play)

Child to fashionable lady visitor: "Your hair smells." — "Not of cooking, I hope." — "Of perfume." — "Thank God"

"That's the way you talk now (logically, sensibly), but in another minute you'll start bawling"

"You're frustrated." — "Why should I be frustrated? I've got a stack of books on my bedside table and I'm looking forward to reading them"

On the phone: "For God's sake, say a human word, something warm, or at least something cold!" Silence

After masturbating, her body feels to her like that of a strange, puny man with spindly legs

Sulfur-yellow late-afternoon light in the bedroom; I feel like a corpse that has been lying here for some time

Children are calling and I don't feel like answering (autism: despair that has finally settled in for good; as though there were no appropriate language for despair)

Dialogue with myself: "Now you will walk down the street very slowly, maybe that will bring you back to life." — And later: "Why have you suddenly started to run?" — "Precisely because I *can* run"

Being able to imagine, to feel something else, to look forward to other places and other times, being able, in short, to think again—today this strikes me almost as divine grace

Improvement: I had started mistaking strangers on the street for people I know

One child about another: "N. forces himself to laugh to make her laugh"

I almost regret that certain people will die without having killed anyone; they seem born for it

A child's wish—to live on an island

A woman, strong in her solitude

The main thing: not to claim history for myself, not to let myself be defined by history, not to take it as an excuse— despise it in those who hide their personal insignificance behind it—and yet know it, in order to understand people and above all to see through them (my hatred of history as a refuge for be-nothings)

"Yesterday was a utopian day"

This evening, after a long dark day, I felt that the self is an (intrinsically) unreliable machine for setting the world in motion; as though the self had to be set in motion (like a power plant) before the world could be illumined (enlightened)

The joy of being able to think for at least a few minutes a day; as though the prerequisite were a long and painful thoughtlessness (deprivation of thought)

Moments: to step outside after nightfall, after the lights have gone on, and to breathe

December

For fear of forgetting my insights, learn not to repeat formulations of them, not even to myself; formulation as a way of forgetting

Sometimes I have no other thought than a pattern (a carpet pattern, for instance) dancing before my eyes

The pathetic cry of a child in a distant corner—she has to go so badly. The Satanic impulse not to answer but to wait and see what will happen

A neighbor received frequent visits from friends who announced their presence with an auto horn that imitated the mooing of a cow. One day my neighbor's child died, and that afternoon his friends came to pay a condolence call. As usual, they announced themselves with the cow horn, but blew it more softly

Hatred of people who bed their sunglasses in their hair

I am usually too lucid to be sad

The fat I'm gagging on: Austria

"I must insist on what, in spite of everything, I manage to be now and then: that is my dignity"

"I'm so fond of you today"

"How are you?" — "I've started playing the pinball machines again"

"I waited two days for someone to say a kind word to me. Then I left the country"

"Your writing is elitist." — "How can anyone who has experienced American movies be elitist?"

The cranky old woman at the newsstand, the park in the soft subdued light, the ugly mug of the lady walking her dog—*I* am all these

A child whistling; at last, after years of trying, the skill has been acquired

Do one thing after another as lucidly as possible: smell the bread, smell the schnapps, fold the paper—therein lies salvation

The housewife: "What makes me so tired is going back and forth, stopping, turning around, turning around again—if I could only keep going straight ahead—for hours"

Hardly anyone writes me a letter, hardly anyone phones; they all seem to have got lost this fall

Maybe the only way of ever feeling closer to that foreign worker would be to quarrel with him in as physical a way as possible

To get home with the shopping and stow the edibles in the refrigerator with the feeling that now I'm all set for a few days (how one gets to be an obsessive hoarder)

By resisting her tenderness, I destroyed our beauty

The interviewer said to the "lonely man": "Tell me about loneliness!" No answer

The woman in Truffaut's film faints; the woman in Godard's film masturbates

I was angry at her for not being what I wanted

Show what it means to be alone (for instance, when the doorbell rings and once again it's only a child)

A woman is with one man and longs for another; but her longing has been awakened, provoked, caused by the one she is with

Gum-chewing girls wandering around the Paris Métro stations

"Dearest, even in my thoughts I can't get through to you"

The insensibility of an athlete after exertion; made heartless by extreme physical effort and the enthusiasm that went with it

Really alive? A glance will tell you

1 9 7 6

January

The pale, made-up woman with the hat in the café. At last someone speaks to her, and being-spoken-to gives her her first moment of calm in all this long day

The husband says something about his rights. The wife: "Don't drag politics into it"

"Often, after I've been with someone, I take pride in the thought that I haven't revealed anything of myself"

The woman sits with her eyes closed. The child: "Are you thinking?" — "No, I'm watching images; they appear when I exhale." The child tries it

In the afternoon they sit in the cafés, staring as if they were already looking at television

Her face in the mirror, the one she uses for daydreaming

Those policemen on patrol: Why don't they strike me down right away? Why do they wait for a motive?

"What are you thinking about?" — "I'm thinking that I wouldn't want to die just now"

"Woman, I'm your friend" (Jeremiah Johnson)

Looking at people, the thought: They are living as though there had been no catastrophe

Joy at the thought of a thoroughly rational world: a perfect rectangle

Tense, unnerved, and close to madness before writing—and when I read what I've written it looks so calm

Proud of my near-madness, as if I had attained a goal

Invent a machine that will relieve me of speaking when I'm spoken to, that will answer for me

People who don't lose their tempers, said D., are easy to insult

At present I welcome opportunities to line up somewhere and wait (at the post office, for instance)

Give no sign of recognition when someone from the neighborhood passes me on the street: I greeted *him* yesterday

How often I feel that I know only the wrong people

At the moment of supreme pleasure, the certainty of having failed once again to attain true pleasure (while the pleasure is still present: "That *was* wonderful!")

She says to someone who accosts her: "Men are always so available!"

Her quick firm gait. Someone asks her: "Do you walk like that to keep from being molested?"

Your deliberately hesitant speech—as if you wanted me to agree in advance

The beautiful young girl: already she listens with knitted brows, as if she had years of experience behind her

Sense of doom at the sight of rubber plants

February

As if pain had no past

The moment I start to write, a centrifugal force sets in (away from the things that "really happened"); the urge to go where people are still alive

How dull to be awake, and how much duller to sleep, even *with* dreams; but sometimes there's a living sleep, without dreams

His "discoveries": "I've *discovered* a new restaurant!"

A writer—or anyone else—who had solved the problem of being alone would cease to interest me

Why should enjoyment of one thing prevent me from enjoying something else?

Children, giggling and whispering, creep up while I am asleep, to frighten me; meanwhile, I think of death—as if they were creeping up on a corpse

A chestnut bud that failed to open last spring, small, hard, shriveled; and now suddenly, on a sunny day in February, it falls to the ground with a soft thud; the impulse to prod myself with it, to hurt myself

I said to her: "One gets the impression that you can do everything!"

Someone watching television said: "Why does there have to be news every day?"

Driving through a dreary suburban countryside on a Sunday afternoon: think a somersault into it and it becomes bearable

There was a puddle in the street; clouds drifted across it, and the sky was blue. A few snowflakes fell into the puddle and floated on the surface without melting. Suddenly time stood still. In my dream that struck me as salvation

"The good old days when I kept forgetting to wind the clocks!"

March 1

Suddenly, in the midst of all the people who crowded around me or spoke to me, I felt as if there were a dead chicken in my chest

This evening I got back from Austria and Germany. Suddenly, at the dark Porte de la Muette on the edge of the Bois de Boulogne, it seemed to me that my life—a kind of second, secret biography—was simultaneously continuing back home in southern Carinthia, continuing very concretely before the eyes of the villagers, and that my body at that moment was painfully, yet almost consolingly stretched over the length and breadth of Europe, that I became a standard of measurement and lost myself

March 2

"What did your dilemma turn into in your dream this time?"

On our return to the big city, I smelled the child's ski cap: it smelled of dried snow water

As though night were falling in my head

March 3

A spider appeared in the middle of the conversation; after it had been hunted and killed, the conversation resumed

A loveless day, without drifting clouds; unclear branches against a shapeless sky—like hostile animals; the whole vast sky as a defect of vision

"I want to hear your opinion." — "My opinion!" she cried in horror

March 4

Always asking the child the same question: "Has anything happened?"

People were moving among the faraway tree trunks in the yellow, obliquely hovering afternoon light; they, too, seemed to hover

Black dejection; and yet the feeling that a triumph is imminent (often toward evening)

March 5

When I awoke, my hair rested on my head like someone's hand

A friend told me he hadn't beaten his children, only stepped on their feet

Fear of death makes his legs shorter

What yesterday was a beautiful substance is today vegetating inside me as mere formal reality

The china dish that has been out of doors all winter: how cold it is!

To walk in the street where for a few steps all is quiet—as though these were the last moments

How slowly the people are walking today, in the warm sun of this supernatural afternoon

A woman approaches in the distance; before distinguishing her features, I catch the sparkle of her earrings

The child said: "I like to make things nobody can recognize" (when I complained that I couldn't tell what her drawing represented)

The beauty of the world today is unbearable for one person alone, even for two; possibly three might endure it

To grow older without the time passing

At the bakery they gave the other customers paper to wrap their bread in, but not the North African

At the news of my friend's death, I saw the world as a room that he had left

After his funeral: inside, as in a garage, lies his body with his hair still mussed from dying; outside, in the gutter, the ash of *his* cigarette is whirling around

Beautiful: a woman who doesn't remind me of anything (of a swan's neck, for instance)

A book that I have a sense of reading with pleasure even when I'm only glancing at it absentmindedly

Two people were talking about a photograph and grabbing it out of each other's hands to look at it, each for himself

"When you say I look sad, it's only to disarm me"

Watching him undress, she talked about his body

March 6

F.: Everything makes her shriek—with horror or ecstasy; and a moment later she forgets all about it

Someone wants to borrow money from me to start a business with. He talks too fast, too much—like a crook

To keep walking straight ahead with this kind of sun on my skin

The rustling green garden in the early morning; every single leaf is shaking; a few, at the ends of the branches, are gradually turned a lighter, almost transparent green, not yet by the direct sun, but by a foregleam of the approaching sunlight. Just as in the first light of day the sky seemed overcast and then, high in the gray sky, the vapor trail of an airplane glittered—showing that up there the sun was shining and that the sky was not overcast but clear and cloudless—so now there are sun spots on the garden wall, but these are only reflections from somewhere else where the sun is already shining. A pigeon flies up to the roof, and at the same time the roar of a motorcycle is heard from the road, as though the pigeon had made this noise in rising. And now the child wakes up. One of her hands is asleep

The feeling that almost everything I have seen or heard up to now loses its original form the moment it enters into me, that it can no longer be directly described in words or represented in images, but is instantly metamorphosed into something quite formless; as though the effort of my writing were needed to change the innumerable formless pupae inside me into something essentially different. Thus, writing would be an awakening of thousands of unformed pupate experiences to new forms, which, however, through my feeling, would still retain a connection with the original experiences—with those authentic, real, but meaningless things, which would thus be the mythological images of my consciousness and my existence; the thought that now arises of all the innumerable, terrifyingly formless pupate hybrids within me, neither thing nor image, but halfway between—and of the work that lies ahead of me to fixate in speech and idea these hybrids (which are only in *being*, without speech or idea, and have not yet started, like embryos, for example, to *become*) and to fashion them into something radiantly new, in which, however, one senses the old, the original experience, as one senses the caterpillar in the butterfly!

A film entitled *My Life*: a long strip of black film in which now and then something flares up; for instance, the hard, withered leaves which in January—when the trees have long been bare—suddenly go skittering across the dry, clean asphalt

Someone is coming to see me: I'd better try not to imagine what it will be like

"How are you?" — "I don't know. I think I'm going mad"

Shaken by sheer existence—as though by a self-generated, causeless movement (when it's over, he picks his nose)

Take my head between my hands—show myself a tenderness

Don't eat carrots—they kill your desire for anything else

Dilemma: insistence on thought has thrown me off it

This afternoon I walked in circles in the park; now it's evening and I'm walking in circles at home

I'm expecting a visit. The moment my visitor rings the doorbell, the life storms that are almost suffocating me will give way to a gigantic blandness. What then is the specter that haunts me: the comforting dullness that will enter with the visitor, or my insignificance when I am alone? Is it not true that my bit of reality will vanish when my visitor comes in and that absolute unreality, the pure specter, will take over in the presence of his touchingly protuberant eyes? —In any case, he will come in any minute now, reeling perhaps and shaken out of his wits by a life storm similar to mine; just what I have said will happen, I shall have to grin like mad, and so perhaps will he

The child's hair: not a smell; from the first moment, a feeling

Sometimes the child becomes alien to me—but only what I love best can become *so* alien

Alone in the night, I winked at myself

After a phone call he noticed that he had written the words "too much" on a slip of paper, though those words had not occurred in the conversation

Why do I sometimes gain self-assurance and peace of mind by attacking others, by flaying them with words, laying them bare, chiding, demolishing them?

The danger of being alone, of all this thinking, pondering, "soul-searching," etc., is that one loses one's capacity for opening up to others

Put up a sign outside my house with the warning: "Caution! Man reading!"

How much there still was to intimidate me ten years ago! Concrete poetry, Andy Warhol, Marx, Freud, structuralism! Now all these Universal Pictures have faded out, and *no one* should feel oppressed by anything but the weight of the world

Toward midnight, the firm round armrest of the sofa looks to me like the fuselage of a plane about to take off

March 7

At daybreak the birds fly past the window on a slant, like falling autumn leaves (confusion in waking)

I said to A.: "You're experiencing so many things that I didn't." — "But you experienced the war!" — "Would you have wanted that?" — "Yes!"

A. said: "I don't like N., and she doesn't like me; but she doesn't want me to know she doesn't like me"

Sitting still in the cold, I finally feel inside me a spot of warmth, which gradually, by dint of my keeping perfectly still, spreads until I feel warm all over

In this sunlight I speak almost tonelessly, as if I were afraid of disturbing something

Sunday sounds in the sunny garden: the clatter of dishes, the jangling of knives and forks from the open windows all around; scissors cutting paper; and now of course the sound of a plane in the distance

The young leaves; the sun shines through them, and now and then the shadows of other leaves move over them

People seem to do everything more and more slowly, thoughtfully, considerately, quietly in the spring sun

The child's ear under her hair in the shadow

Suddenly the wind in the big city sounds like a storm in a mountain forest

Sunlit hair flying, as branches with their luminous buds fly in the sunlight; the present has become inhumanly painful

On sunlit leaves the shadows of other leaves; sometimes, when the whole bush is in motion, the shadows tremble with the leaves; sometimes (when just this one branch moves) only the sunlit leaves emerge from the shadows and tremble; sometimes only the shadows of the other leaves tremble on the motionless sunlit leaves

In opening my eyes I held my hand in front of them, as one does before one's mouth when picking one's teeth—as though there were something repulsive about this difficult eye opening

"At last I feel better—I feel earthbound again"

It would be nice to look out the window, but I'm inhibited by this woman watching me

To yearn for stupidity as for a home port

The taste of blood in my mouth reminded me instantly of a long-past love (of a woman I once loved)

I have to admit it, I find most people bearable only when I'm attacking them!

So she has come for a visit in spite of her preposterous short hair, what impudence; and she always clears her throat before speaking; and she stumbles on the stairs; and she keeps getting in my way, so we're always bumping into each other; and on the pretext that she's "company," she expects me to be available at all times—when I want so much to be alone (and here I am again in an absurd no-man's-land between solitude and companionship, neither alone nor really with someone else)

A teacher like her will send hundreds and hundreds of un-languaged figures like herself out into the world, and each one of these in turn will produce hundreds and thousands of dumpling eaters

Here she is beside me, suffering in silence, draining my existence

Sometimes in her sleep the child stops breathing for seconds at a time

The "unknown companion." With her there would not be the usual initial difficulties; for instance, the question of: I to her, or she to me? Neither, in his accustomed place, would feel disturbed by the other's coming from somewhere else, as I can't help feeling now with this "former girl friend," when I see strange tubes, bracelets, etc., in "my" bathroom

I'm glad I feel no pity for her; this way she preserves her dignity, her independence

As she was fighting back the tears, her carotid stood out

And her preposterous navy-blue coat with its hood and bamboo buttons!

I look in some other direction and feel that she is looking at me. So now I can neither go on looking where I wanted nor turn to her; I feel that part of my body is paralyzed; and my eyes, aware of this paralyzing gaze, are strangely blinded; only a last congealed image lies dead on my eyeballs, as though painted

A writer has written: if not for her (his life's companion), he would have written no books, he'd have "pushed a baby carriage"

James Joyce had a vocabulary of thirty thousand words; that's what makes him the most important writer of this century

One more number in the hit parade of idiocy: a writer who has stopped writing (and as usual wants in self-defense to impose non-writing upon others as a norm) finds it backward that writers are again beginning to describe their dreams instead of going to a psychoanalyst and having their dreams explained away

In talking with this woman, I must take care not to think, after every sentence, that I've told her off again! (I must take care that our conversation doesn't become a duel)

The way she bends her fingers backward (memory of my schooldays)! Like a child—but those long, red fingers with their poor circulation!

If I saw her at her daily work, she would be herself again, and I'd be able to look at her impersonally, but with respect

The shadow of the pigeon tripping about on the glass roof of the railroad station: the shadow moves as if the body were coming toward me, while in reality it's moving away

This woman is too easily pleased for one to wish to be her lover

When you ask her if she wants something—regardless of what it is—she answers at once: "Oh, yes!"

She hasn't heated the teapot! And she put so much water in the kettle that now, fifteen minutes later, it hasn't yet begun to boil. And the way she taps the salt shaker! —Sitting at the table with her, I long to tell her to clear out. This minute!

She's so terrified of me that she hums the whole time

Then she left me and read *Asterix* with the child for hours; that probably gave her a feeling of humanity after my malignant presence

And to top it all, her stupid new shoes have started squeaking again!

All of a sudden I'm beginning to hate her

How cramped the three of us are in the cab. I could scream, because with her beside me I can hardly reach into my pocket for money

She touches me only lightly, only accidentally, and for a moment I think I'm suffocating

What a blessing after that to be able to look peacefully at an advertising poster!

A blind man was walking very slowly and awkwardly in front of me, and I thought: Only someone who went blind *recently* would walk like that

What makes me so irritable is that I love someone I don't know and *am* with someone I know and am not in love with; I feel like giving everyone a kick

Then she asks me: "Is the food good here?" —And she does everything I do, butters her bread, sprinkles salt on the butter. The second I risk a movement, she imitates it

I ordered a beer I didn't want and asked her insidiously if she'd like one, too; naturally, she blinked and nodded

For the first time in ages I bit my tongue

Suddenly I thought: I really wouldn't want to stick my noble cock into such a woman! I smiled at her dreamily, and she smiled back

Two people staring at each other in a suburban train: an elderly foreign working woman and a young foreign writer, neither a friendly nor a hostile stare. After quite some time, the writer averted his eyes—as though his whole history forbade him to stare at this woman any longer; as though the only thing he could possibly do was yield to her

To avoid the euphoria that threatened me, I took a deep breath

The big cup of steaming tea lay in my lap like a cat

Now she's started making herself useful, hammering all over the house

Slipped on the ice but didn't fall: after long, steady walking, it gave me a wonderful feeling, my legs being wrenched apart, the fear, and then going on with my walk

Out of the corner of my eye, I saw the woman only as movement, as chewing

But in taking leave, she said something splendid: "You think people like me should have their noses held, don't you?"

When I opened the door for her, we both had a good laugh

And in the end of course pity is unavoidable

Not yet being able to write *everything*: a comforting feeling (to know you'd stop at *something*)

She looked at me with the childish sadness of a hopelessly high-strung woman

"A bitter, masculine anger stirred within him at the destructive emotionalism of these women, unable, as they always were, to 'leave well alone'" (John Cowper Powys, *Wolf Solent*)

March 8

I always ruin my pillows by crushing and flattening them beyond recognition; it's just my way of sleeping

In spite of my bad humor, I've been singing the silliest songs imaginable, and after a while I notice that the silly stuff I'm singing has driven away my bad humor

Idea of a sexual "encounter": we would both concentrate on just that—and yet, though wholly in the grip of sensuality, she would expect me to give her that one glance that would change everything

In the gray of dawn, the bird sounds are still unconnected

If only I could get rid of the loathing and rage that sounds inspire in me! I'm thinking of the sounds of my childhood, which split my head, the sounds my father made gulping down liquor, his way of smacking his lips; the muffled clashing of his teeth even when he was spooning up soup; his smoker's cough in the toilet on damp cold mornings; or our neighbor with his perpetual little hacking cough, his sons promised to thrash him if he didn't stop (he has it to this day)—all these sounds, my mother's screaming sneeze that could be heard at the other end of the village, the affected little kitten-sneeze of an aunt (in comparison to which my mother took pride in her way of sneezing), my grandfather's way of puffing through his nose when playing cards, the universal body-scratching, the click-click-click of nails being cut in the living room, the ubiquitous belching, my mother's hiccups (so frequent that they made her cry), my father's mixture of Berlin and Carinthian dialect (my distaste for all dialects), his voice in general, without emphasis, without conviction, a cowardly voice, so to speak, in all possible situations (that's how it struck me then in my hate), even when he was screaming and yelling in his drunkenness, the glug-glug of stinking liquor being poured into glasses or directly down throats, which didn't even need to swallow, the heavy breathing of old women at the table— I know, I know, there are explanations—but even so, there are nights when I could burst with rage, when I could scream and bash my head against the wall; for instance, when my own child swallows her saliva in her sleep: misery

A ride on the Métro, looking at all the closed-in people in the car. The sudden thought: How grateful we silent people here underground would have reason to be if someone should suddenly start talking about himself without reserve, if someone should lay himself bare in speech

My love for A. is so strong that I long for a conflict between us, because then I could prove my love for her without the nervousness that comes over me in our present conflictless state

In the morning my cold hands are made even colder by the things I take out of the refrigerator

That woman wheezes while eating, and sputters at the mouth, as women do who have been living alone a long time

Just once, when I laid the bank note on the waiter's salver, the woman, who had been talking without interruption, looked at me for a moment out of the corner of her eye

And if, while I'm stopping my ears against her talk-sounds, she were to ask me what was the matter, I would only be able to give her a silent, murderous look

All day someone has been sitting next to me, on both sides of me, and across from me. I have to pull in my feet, cramp my arms, and read the newspaper folded

Sense of awkwardness when my feelings are unclear

Someone who, while standing in a bus, at last finds the rhythm of his sadness, joins willingly in the movements of the bus, the street, his fellow passengers

In the midst of the big-city traffic, even during the evening rush hour, there is a sudden lull, when all you can hear is the sound of the window being closed, and then the noise starts in again

The child wants to give me her hand, because her dangling arm bothers her

The sudden thought that war would soothe me, by turning my inside outside; I'd have no more trouble with time and unreality: an unreal thought!

Sometimes, in silent soliloquies, I speak rhetorically to myself

Sweet kitchen melancholy; I sit stiffly in the kitchen, drinking wine, the dishwater from the upper stories runs peacefully through the pipes; now it's stopping; too bad!

A woman tell me she "pities" me; she meant it as an aggression, of course

An idea: for me the waking state is already dream work, so there's nothing for my dreams to work on and they can play freely

To look an enemy in the eye and make him stop conceding, changing the subject, minimizing, getting friendly ("Personally, I like you" and suchlike abominations)

"Are you disgusted with me?" — "No, I knew what to expect"

March 9

In any number of my stories I meant to send my heroes to the seashore for a little intermezzo, but it never worked out that way!

Something that upsets my balance: my mind is often a little ahead of whatever action I am performing; this brief moment of cleavage between consciousness and activity sometimes impedes my feeling for the activity (e.g., washing in cold water, walking, running, eating; or writing, for that matter!)

Viewing Chartres cathedral. In the town afterwards, in a street that was almost countrified, I looked up at the spires on the hill and then down to the canal at my feet. The water was almost stagnant, covered with dense green duckweed, which thinned a little now and then. How good it felt, after looking up so long at the cathedral, to look down at the gently drifting duckweed!

Amazing how many of the stores around here have folded in the time I've been here, how many owners have died, how many of the menus outside restaurants are written in a different hand, though the dishes are still the same

The sleeping child's thumb is moving

More about these upsets in my balance: A moment before I actually do something, e.g., look at the child, I *play* at doing it, I do a pantomime of looking-at before actually looking at her, a pantomime of laughing before laughing out loud. This lack of simultaneity often impedes my feeling and gives my premature play laughter an unfeeling quality (which can also be observed in most other people); the fact that I express something before my feeling for it is wholly present gives this expression an affected, sanctimonious quality; and this getting ahead of myself, this mental anticipation, also makes me break my ties with the earth and rise up into a painful void; this accounts for my compulsive way of smelling things—in order to keep them with me, to enable me to stay with them instead of being catapulted out into the void

To keep from crying, a child stares at the school satchels hanging in the cloakroom

I look up from long newspaper reading, during which my mind is neither on what I am reading nor elsewhere, and see the blue sky outside and the crowns of the plane trees swinging and swaying—the world opens before my eyes

The people sit chatting in the sunny suburban bus, while waiting for it to start; people who travel together every day, not silent solitary figures starting on a train trip

The old woman apologizes to the driver for boarding his bus by mistake

Old women walking on the edge of the road at night in Austria

This girl on the bench at the bus stop is sure to have seen lots of men walking furtively back and forth in front of her

On the bus: "Heavenly!" —At this thought I see my face reflected in the windshield: a gloomy face

A plane coming in for a landing flies low over the bus, wavering, as though pilotless, as though its course were being constantly revised by someone on the ground, as though a deviation were being constantly corrected

The workers on the railroad tracks—all seem to be without rank, no boss or leader or top man—they make faces at each other and jostle one another and then they grin

March 10

The living green of the leaves outside, almost as though there were swarms of glittering insects on the tree, green butterflies of unknown nature, and suddenly the whole garden becomes an *unknown nature*; and in the room I suddenly see a blossom, which fell intact during the night, lying on the floor, no longer recognizable as a blossom, turned to shards and ashes; another unknown nature, moth wings mingled with specks of beetle shells, now indefinable

This wineshop really smells as if some of the wine were uncorked and people drank it right here on the premises

The old man in the restaurant: he holds his empty wine bottle over his glass until the last drop detaches itself (feeling of a self-portrait)

I looked into the street sweeper's face and saw he was looking at me, and for the first time, with surprise, we greeted each other, and now we shall have to keep on greeting each other

A man bends over a child as though wanting to give it mouth-to-mouth resuscitation

A collection of my *idées fixes*: that A. suddenly stops growing; that I'm riding down in an elevator, reflecting that my chances of survival, in case the elevator should crash, are increasing from floor to floor; that I'm passing a gasoline truck and wondering how far I have to go to be out of the danger zone in case it explodes; that death overtakes me in the bathroom where it is warm; that I die while shitting; that I must take care to switch on the light with my right hand, because an electric shock on the left side goes straight to the heart; that the funicular cable snaps over the deepest chasm, etc.

Suppose someday in a busy store I make no move to show it's my turn; I won't even look around, but just stand still and wait to see if I ever get waited on

What bitterness I felt today toward myself and the world when, as I was standing in line for the swing at the playground, a child tried to slip in ahead of me and I had to tell him it was *my* child's turn; my awareness of this child's unhappiness and defenselessness filled me with such bitterness and rage at everything in the world that I wanted to slap A., who was swinging so unenthusiastically—bitterness, despair, sense of failure, wretchedness, misery, and now, as I write it down, at least sadness

On a city square, four men were standing around a manhole. One kept shouting down: "Pull the rope!" and another held the rope, which remained slack. But the men were perfectly calm, they kept calling down quite calmly; in fact, the longer they called and the longer the rope remained slack, the calmer they became—as though it still amused them to suppose that something might actually have happened. It now seemed quite possible that something had gone wrong, but the idea was still absurd. At the same time, the men's calm was a means of reassuring one another, a kind of rigid calm, prepared for an impending paroxysm of fear—an uncalm calm

A strange idea struck me in the kitchen as I unwrapped the fragrant white butter and smelled it and peeled the first little radishes of the season, and raised them, too, to my nose: the idea that with such gestures we conjure up the smells of our childhood, though such objects can never have been so close to our noses in those days; now we have to hold these things close to our faces if we want to smell and feel something which in childhood permeated us without any need to pick it up. Have the smells grown weaker? (That, too, no doubt.) Or is it our sense of smell? (That, too, no doubt.) —In any case, what in those days we "just" took as it came, we must now purposely, intentionally, deliberately bring close to us (actually I meant to write something different, my idea in the kitchen was much more complicated; the essential was not the explanations—things are not as fragrant, our sense of smell has deteriorated—but the instant thought that in childhood everything was in its place and I perceived it all the same, while now I have to remove so many things from their place, displace them, be hurt by them, in order to perceive them)

When I hit rock bottom and stop caring one way or the other, shortly before I die for good, I shall become a member of society (no matter which)

I regret to say that I have not yet become totally unrecognizable, totally inconspicuous

When someone wants something of me on the telephone, I say: "Let me think it over for a few days." And I don't think it over for one second

Deep night; all the people in my life seem present to me; if anyone should come to me now, no matter who, I should be ready for him, available to him, wonderfully understanding; yet I would still be in full possession of myself

"What are you doing right now?" — "I'm gazing into space, letting myself drift into the universe"

The chest of drawers stands with legs outspread like an old woman

In front of the mirror at midnight: I can still see (I haven't gone blind), my heart is still beating

Suddenly having a bed of my own, lying under a blanket, being able to choose a position to lie in has—once again—ceased to be self-evident

An image: empty human cocoons drifting like cigarette butts along the roads of the earth

March 11

How empty my sleep was! Over and over again, while sleeping, I realized how empty my sleep was, and a headache set in; then something happened, the headache was gone, and I had a feeling of inexplicable fulfillment, but it was only that the emptiness was gone

I was proud: at last I was witnessing a murder

My feeling of self, which isolates my own self, is also the source of my feeling for others, whom I see as equally isolated, and that in turn brings me close to them

The child describes her day with me as follows: "Today C. came over. She brought L. with her. Now they've gone and I'm all alone with ——, who is in the kitchen playing music while he works. Today I threw the record player on the floor, but it didn't break. Then I showed —— my notebook, and he said he would look at it when he finished working. Now I think the music is kind of sad"

Describe a successful day

Learn to live outside the consciousness, opinions, conceptions of others

When I look at myself, I think perhaps I have a right to be afraid, but I should stop talking about it

A passing barge has several piles of sand on it; on one of them a shepherd dog stands motionless

At first, when I look at the opposite bank, I see only "bright-colored rectangular objects." I have to make an effort to recognize first bricks and then piles of washbasins covered with shiny plastic

In this pissoir with its yellow tiles my eyes have been opened for the first time today

Perceptions on the way home, unintentional: the rubber bands on the wrist of the salesgirl in the gourmet food shop; at the sight of a brown department-store bag on the back seat of a car, it flashed through my mind that this was my bag (so much a part of daily life has this kind of bag become); a woman eating bread on the street kept dropping crumbs, which gleamed like drops of water in the light of the low-lying sun

By naming presents they have given her, I remind the child of people she would otherwise not remember; then she remembers at once

A woman on an upper story of a house was closing the shutters in broad daylight; I looked up at her and our glances met like those of momentary accomplices

I sit facing someone with the old-new idea that *obviously* I ought to be one with that person; how can we possibly be two, each for himself, sitting face to face?

My hatred of "Mr. Unknown" when the doorbell rings

If someone looked in and saw me now, at about midnight, he would see a man standing at an open ground-floor window, in an apartment strangely ramified by mirrors, a man obliged to lead a completely novelistic life (and what's more, I want to)

Nearly all the lights are out, and only occasionally, when someone switches on the light in the courtyard, does a pale latticework of light fall into the apartment, which, with all its mirrors, oval and round, and with all its doors open, is now a very special theatrical place

March 12

Waking from sheltered sleep: like being tripped up while taking a quiet stroll

Waking with the thought that I've strangled the child; not daring to reach out and touch her; at last a sigh beside me

Ruins of memory: I try to remember the details of places, houses, faces, and all I see is ruins

Powdered sugar on my shoes from eating doughnuts (Austria)

The sensation of moving about like a sleeper who wants to look at the clock and in his dreams does indeed keep looking at the clock (because he has to get up soon), but never actually does look at the clock

If I could only look calmly at someone who hates me

A beggar holds out his hand in front of me and I shake my head angrily because he has put me into such a situation (other people just turn away in indifference)

People who have what's needed for every emergency: umbrella, aspirin, etc.

A girl who for once does not ooze tears in that well-behaved way but lets the corners of her mouth droop and bawls out loud

The salesgirl in an empty shop that stays open at lunch hour is dreamily munching a sandwich (I wrote this outside the open shop door, which someone closed at that very moment)

The teacher who had just taken the children to the farm show (bus ride, street crossings) told me she was always in a bad humor on days when she was going to have to take the children out; at the beginning of the school year, she said, she refused to take them anywhere until she knew all about each one of them, their way of walking, etc.

The sheep at the farm show breathed mechanically, like pumps: it's their sense of doom that turns them into machines

"What would you like to accomplish by writing?" — "To make people laugh and cry" (I imagine being able to say such things in all seriousness)

Years ago, someone said the nice thing about me was that I had no habits. And now?

People are always claiming to be a mixture of "good and bad"; as for me, I am either all good or all bad

Nice, seeing my child with other children, as if she belonged with them

That day a pale, solemn, unknown child came in out of the rain with other children, and I didn't recognize her as my own: horror, and at the same time marvel

March 13

Interrupted in her thoughts of never-never land as she lies abed in the morning, A. says: "Now let me go on thinking!"

Strange how often I use the conditional when speaking French

The salesgirl gave me too much change; while she was still holding out a bank note, I hoped she wouldn't notice her mistake, because then I'd be able to show her how honest I am

My balance between madness and philistinism

Herr F. said: "I saw my wife standing in the street, with nothing but the sky over her, like the subject of a photograph. Maybe that's why I told her to *smile*"

Conceivable duel: A. doesn't want to die before B. (the duel consists in their trying to outlive each other)

Longing for a river

As I walked on after ducking my head in the brook, I felt sand between my teeth

To have managed to do something once and never succeed in doing it again

A. combing her hair in the bathroom, elated though alone— I can conceive of a child as alone yet alive, soaring above all thoughts of loneliness—of myself no longer

"It's not a pain, only a complaint"

In the evening, birds flutter unseen in the bushes, but they don't fly away

Long after nightfall, there is still that bright stripe in the dark sky; it has been there quite some time; the thought that it will never go away, an eternal bright stripe in the night sky, an epiphany for all time

The coming of spring in the country—the tiny indications vanish in the general bleakness of a no-man's-land; while in the city it's there, you can see it happening

March 14

Dream of going blind: iris and pupil fade, dissolve in the gray-white eyeball, like curdling milk

The joyful state when you forget to breathe and the most you can manage is a long sigh from time to time

Triumphant thought: I have a history! And I will continue to have one!

About Austria: I never identify the people I love best there with the country!

What if the only sounds to be heard in the country were the cries of pain of peacocks, donkeys, chickens, and pigs; there would be total war, and the cocks would never stop crowing

Barbed-wire childhood

Behind a window someone is shaking a baby

The dead cars outside the window in the night

March 15

Make the sounds and gestures of an old man—and take pleasure in them

Sometimes the wonderful feeling that I'm living the way I want

The thought that hatters, drapers, etc., mostly from England (—— & Sons), die but do not decay (the thought that if I owned a nice little novelty shop I'd be secure against all eventualities for the rest of my life)

Today time was beautiful (not that I had a "beautiful time"; the beautiful thing was time itself, though nothing especially wonderful happened)

I saw for the first time that the sex act can confer a long-absent dignity (to a woman's face)

Suppose someone who has danced to every tune were to cry out one day: "If only I could finally begin to live!"

Whenever I talk to Herr F. on the phone, Frau F. starts talking in the background (today she was in the shower, but she nevertheless kept shouting something that her husband passed on to me)

"Keep walking until I get out of myself"

The child pointed to her eye, to the place where the afterimage was

"This woman sat there the whole time—and it never even occurred to me that she might be there on my account!"

The bleakest section of the city seemed more hospitable to me than that rural-looking bridle path with the leafless bushes on either side and the yellow Métro map in the gray sand with the hoofprints on it

A human being as a swaying bundle of hair in an ambulance

Often, when I'm shown a picture of myself in a group, I only pretend to look at the others, or I concentrate excessively on details in the other people's pictures

The psychoanalyst sat there, nodding and smiling at what I said, as if I were one of his cases, and for a moment I felt I was telling my story to an expert (but actually I was only trying to be obliging, to make him, in my presence at least, feel like an expert)

Today the sun shone for just one moment: for just that moment, the latticework in the room

Read an article about the mystical experiences of a psychoanalyst: he only claims to have (had) them; if he had really had them, he wouldn't write such jargon, they would have affected his language

"Provided I'm ready, any woman in the world will look at me"

As we (the man, his wife, and I) drove past the cemetery where their child lies buried, it seemed to me, three years after the child's death, that I heard the wife give a deep sigh

March 16

In my half-sleep, images fill my whole skull as singing fills a church

A.'s nightmare: a third arm growing out of my back

This woman's eyes—they don't seem to be part of her face; it's as though there were an old, scarred face behind her broad young one, and as though these deep-set, tiny, almost square eyes belonged to the old face; they seemed to be moving behind cutouts in a mask

The church seems to offer the most superficial and at the same time the most profound consolation—you enter and it shelters you along with all the other people; no one presumes to address you personally or listen to you personally (as in psychoanalysis)

A man with a flushed red face walked slowly past me and suddenly tried to trip me—afterwards I was glad

While watching that stupid film, I felt that I'd have to be carried out at the end

When I asked her "Have you a lover?" she answered, "I don't want anything from you"

Outside the café, the imprints of bottle caps in the asphalt; they were tossed there in the summer, when the asphalt was soft

"Old man, you ought to be ashamed of your dead eyes!"

Maybe when I feel dashing, I only look unapproachable or cross

Someone saw me at the café and said: "So this is your stamping ground!"

A coat with nice deep pockets; a whole loaf of bread can vanish in one of them and reappear like magic

Scream at that fellow with the big yawn

I'm not quick-tempered, that would be an attractive vice; I only lack self-control

One day, when we had gone to a lake to bathe, I was sent to get something out of my uncle's car. In opening the door, I clumsily broke the key. When I got back, covered with shame, my mother said proudly to my uncle: "You see what strength he has in his hands!"

Memory of a lunch with friends a year ago. Though we were all "grown men," we went on and on comparing notes about how often we washed our hair; I remember the sense of profound well-being this endless talk gave me

"After a quick but not hurried kiss" (Katherine Mansfield); after a long, hurried kiss (the longer, the more hurried)

Someone has written me a letter in which he apologizes for not having phoned me instead

My greatness: being alone

March 17

The picture puzzles we often see when looking out the window at random; we see a shape but don't know what it means; today, for instance, I saw a bright stripe on a dark-green awning; at first I thought someone had dropped something from an upper story. Then finally it dawned on me. During the rainstorm last night the wind had turned up part of the overhanging fringe of the awning, which had stuck to the wet canvas, and this was what looked like a light-colored stripe. Make a collection of one day's picture puzzles

For each one of my sentences the psychoanalyst used a code, which, however, was only part of another ready-made linguistic system; what needs to be done: desystematize all ready-made linguistic systems, stop inventing codes, decodify those already in existence

As I passed the bank, a man was just getting out of an armored truck. He took out his revolver and looked me straight in the eye; his look was deep and wide, and I was certain that he was prepared to kill me at the first false move

When angry, she talks like a machine

How often I have felt that women were enemies—and yet it gives me a lift to go about the streets among women I don't know

A book (*Wolf Solent*) that I read as though it had something to teach me for all the rest of my life

How proud I am of being alone! For instance, if someone comes to see me and someone else is already there, I explain at once that the someone else just happened to drop in

Katherine Mansfield: "What will happen to Anatole France and his charming smile? Doesn't it disguise a lack of feeling, like M.'s weariness?" (Mine, too, sometimes)

As beautiful as an animal grown old (e.g., a horse)

People I will never be able to save, not even by the most forceful calm, from their terrible knowingness, their unseemly freedom from illusions

Someone drops something and I pull my hand out of my pocket, but that's all I do

As though all beauty had come into being because of a woman who existed only in dreams

March 18

F.: While you are doing something (reaching for a glass, walking, limping), she tells you what you are doing and what it means (in her opinion); she even knows what you feel at the time

Images in half-sleep: they alone exist, there is no longer any inside or outside; as feeling, they fill all space, and I, in this feeling, am sheltered; it is a feeling that requires no further specification: just plain "feeling"

My dislike of disorder created by others in my accustomed surroundings; my hatred of smells that do not originate with me

As if form were not rooted in experience (of reality)

Someone who makes himself at home in my place the moment he arrives; the television is too loud for him, the color too bright; he wanders around, yawning and stretching—and the worst of it is that all the time he's here I am unable to see, hear, feel anything else

The feeling that I have a fate! And am master of it!

"If I can't help myself, then no one else can help me"

I force myself to write about something I don't believe in, because I don't want to be restricted to this self of mine that does not believe in the something else—maybe if I describe it patiently, I'll come to believe in it

The more intimately A. and I live together, the more unreal, the more unfathomable she sometimes becomes to me

In an old Jean Renoir film, little white clouds go racing across the sky behind Notre Dame, and I thought: Those clouds moved across the sky more than forty years ago

This person who phones every day and hangs up when I answer—maybe he just wants to make sure I'm still alive; maybe he does it out of concern for me, and not to bother me

An elderly gangster; the hairs in his ears look like iron filings clustered around a magnet, or like a big burr

A woman with cold eyes in an impassive face walked past me: I can conceive of her only with that look—or biting into something

Mornings I will practice doing whatever I do as far as possible without speaking, only with silent signs; maybe with no other sign than my mere presence

The station on the edge of the city is lit only by the lamps on the street above it; a small night-light is burning in the deserted ticket office; some out-of-towners, who don't know there's a strike on, are standing on the platform in the rain

When the commercials came on at the movies, I turned away and looked at something else, as I did as a child during the kissing scenes, where the man pressed his lips to the woman's chin

Sometimes the feeling that all the advertising slogans and the inescapable headlines of the scandal sheets will someday club me to death

As we were leaving the cinema, the usher was sitting huddled in a corner, sleeping with her mouth open, a pale, skinny young girl wearing a suit from a boutique advertised before the beginning of the film ("Our staff is dressed by . . .")

The certainty that if I am really amiable nothing can happen to me

If someone asks me who I am, I'll show him my passport

The trouble with great literature is that any asshole can identify with it

I saw the woman walking barefoot across the parquet floor, and thought without tenderness of her corpse lying there with bare feet

March 19

That bird sings like someone brushing his teeth in a hurry (and with that sound and that thought I woke up)

Fascists: prematurely arrested longings (their carefully concealed bald heads)

A true metaphor: like everyday reality, transformed into a dream that clarifies it

Her eagerness to listen always tempts me to pretend eagerness to tell her something

Often, when I meet someone, the first sudden moment of recognition is enough for me, and I see nothing more in that person

How much energy is wasted when you get ready to greet someone who is approaching you, and nothing comes of it

Someone who, when asked even the most trifling question, ponders endlessly before answering

How necessary art is to me day after day, if I am not to wish some of the people I love best would die, or kill them with my indifference

A beautiful moment: I was almost moved by the smell of cooking in my apartment (though for once the smell did not originate with me)

"Before ringing at the strange door, I'd like to look around for a moment and think—because in company I won't be able to"

While the men sit there drinking wine, the woman, who is cooking dinner, comes in from time to time and, without sitting down, takes a sip of wine from her glass; she is so free in her movements that each time she goes out into the kitchen the buttons of her open jacket click against the doorframe (sense of shelteredness)

He looks at everything in the unfamiliar apartment, so as to have something new for his dreams

Someone who in speaking makes gestures in advance to go with what he then proceeds to say—that's rhetoric!

Suddenly, toward midnight, while following a discussion on TV, it occurs to me that one might consider this television riffraff with the compassion of Sherwood Anderson writing about the lost small-town folk of Winesburg, Ohio (then at last it would be possible to write about them)

My friend seemed very young this evening, ready for anything, fearless, he hardly scratched himself at all (I've always taken his scratching as a sign of panic)

Passion without lust; lust without passion; let passion grow so strong that all lust vanishes; passion: happiness; lust: unhappiness; lust without passion leads to ugly shyness; passion without lust: freedom that infects even the lecher

A man and a woman are sitting in the dark, turning their heads away from each other, toward each other, away from each other

At last his face, which had been rigid all day, twisted and was beautiful

March 20

I went to her and asked her who she was. Then I embraced her; I felt her whole body and thought: This is the woman for me. —Before that, there had been a sobering moment when she started to tell me who she was. But as soon as I embraced her body, its powerful charm made me feel at one with her. When I awoke, I toyed with the thought of hiring a private detective to search for her. Embracing her body, gathering it into me, I didn't feel the slightest lust—only passion and release

Everybody coddles and caresses him, as if they were afraid of him

At the sight of her, his violently adult, always controlled expression turned into a crooked, childish grin

At the sight of a woman with enormously protuberant eyes, my irritation vanished

Someone's whole life depends on this conversation, but we keep on grinning as if the whole thing were a joke

After speaking (which I can sometimes do), I feel the need of doing something of which I am incapable

A woman with a heavy load is walking in front of me; but she doesn't put it down, so I can't come to her aid

Two people are standing silent side by side on the street, as though they had just quarreled once and for all

I am interrupted while opening a bottle; then I go back to the kitchen and see the corkscrew with its parted arms protruding grotesquely from the top of the bottle, which is all by itself on the table

He said furiously: "We don't speak the same language!" (At last he had understood what I was trying to say)

"Do you still have such dry hands?" — "No complicity, if you please"

The worst thing about pain is that the world around you becomes so unreal that you are no longer able to help

A beautiful, severe, statuesque, cold, enthusiastic woman, who walks bouncingly, and to make matters worse starts singing a revolutionary song. How I hate her!

G.'s apartment: a bright cool room, where I am in my element (as in my childhood when after my bath I'd sit for a while at the table, under the electric light, eating fresh white bread with cinnamon: cleanliness, ease, companionship without conspiracy)

After taking our dead friend's child to live with her, my grandmother warned him against me as if I had been an enemy, and once when I impulsively picked the child up as I had often done before, he didn't resist, but looked frantically in her direction (horror, misery, rage)

When someone spent the evening with me and all we could do was sit there gloomily, each wrapped up in himself, the silence was so lifeless that I thought it would make my visitor think how bad it must be when I am alone; usually, as a matter of fact, when I'm alone in the apartment, the silence is full and living; vibrant with my thoughts

"Now I feel a different pain: the pain of healing"

March 21

This morning when the concierge (a Spaniard) handed me the mail, he tilted his head slightly to one side; at the moment this was a gesture of profound and charming courtesy

In telling someone that I have an appointment with a doctor, lawyer, tax counselor, etc., I take an almost boastful tone—as though wanting to show that I'm "facing up to reality" (I must get rid of these conventional conceptions of "reality")

On coming home from the movies, I tell someone a few details of the picture, as though I owed him an alibi, proof that I hadn't been doing something else

Rediscover the forgotten, anonymous language of all mankind, and it will shine in self-evidence (my task)

What, in the two years that I've been here, have I noticed about the big apartment house across the street? Once there was a party in one of the apartments, and some people were standing on a balcony; once I saw the blue glow of a television screen; once I saw a woman in a turban shaking out a carpet; once a child stood at a window, lowering something on a string to another child

When I asked her how much the cake she brought had cost, she laughed, as though she had been thinking about the same thing

My sense of responsibility (my feeling that I alone am responsible for myself)—which on the other hand favors my guilt feeling

To avoid giving in to these slight daily twinges of sympathy, I set my jaws firmly

When I think about other people, my consciousness, deep inside me, revolves like an insensible machine, slow and all-embracing

The feeling that to recapture the joys of childhood (the first game of marbles in early spring) I would have to become an idiot

People are crossing the open space in the sunlit park down below in different directions, and yet for a moment, because of their short shadows and the hot glaring light, they all seem to belong together

The sun shines on my writing hand and strengthens it

We walk around the huge terrace of the monumental building, from the sunny side to the shady side, from sheltered warmth to cold wind; as though passing through the circuit of seasons (we stand up top in the sheltered warmth, and in the shade down below someone is walking along in an overcoat and a wind-blown muffler)

Her cold hair in the warm sun

The roar of the city, and in the midst of it, barely audible, birds chatter in a tree, a cock crows, a clump of dry grass rustles (the city universe)

Reply to a stupid, insolent remark by slowly raising my head

I make a face involuntarily and they turn away from me, because now they think they know what kind of person I am

My disappointment when the roar I took for the wind turns out to be something else (cars)

A television talk-show host laughs aloud at something, quite spontaneously—but all the same he forces himself to laugh into the mike

An unapproachable woman—interested only in her appearance (and indeed her first appearance is all there is to her)

March 22

The doorbell is ringing violently; whoever it is must be ringing for the second time (with certain long loud rings I know before opening that it's the meter reader, a salesman, or a policeman—anyway, someone who's up to no good)

She attacks me because I'm the only person she can destroy (with the others, with the people who are responsible for her she is powerless, and she has no sense of responsibility for herself)

She said she liked *fantastic* food (which didn't look like real food)

Lying in bed with my fear of death, I try to take refuge in sexual fantasies

The trick (often employed by women) of turning a man into a child or at least bringing out the child in him

March 23

Washing a shirt in the washbasin when all is still and the heart is heavy

The woman's parents had taken her children away from her on the grounds that during her adolescence she had spent some time in a mental institution. (Cause: her parents.) This woman's lawyer (female) kept expressing sympathy, but she was totally indifferent; when the telephone rang, she would answer right in the middle of her effusions of sympathy, as though glad of the interruption. There was an enormous bunch of flowers on the table between her and her client, and both kept having to bend to one side to see each other. The room was bare; only an overloaded table in the center; the window-panes were clouded over. As though in a ritual, the lawyer kept picking up her little legal code, her badge of office; she would leaf through it without reading a single word and mechanically drop a feminist phrase or two. A suicide room

A book written so feverishly one can't help thinking that the author was trying to hide something

Animated cartoon: a unicorn in a treetop, mourning his lost love. It brings tears to my eyes

I evaded evil with my body, though it came from my body

A successful breath

Dying in a highway tunnel (I felt my body expanding)

There was a vase of forsythia in the center of the table. I propped my elbows on the table and saw that the flowers trembled with my heartbeat. When the others propped their elbows on the table, the forsythia didn't stir

In my fear of death I begged her to stay, but she scented death and fled

For a good part of my life I fought off the outside world with all my soul, and now that I think myself open to it, it attacks *my body*

If only this booming, deafening fear of death would become a silent bodily pain, as it was just a moment ago! (I can't hear myself any more)

The cold telephone

What looks to me like a malignant glitter of machines among the people in the park is baby carriages

I notice that in my mortal fear I move with upraised hands and outthrust behind, like some kind of homosexual

To think, even while zipping a zipper, that this will be the death blow

"Oh, stay a while," I said, smiling. "I'm rather frightened"

A bus passes, with the yellow evening sky in its rear window: "It doesn't do anything for me any more!"

And then I washed all the dishes, so nothing unclean would remain (I write about myself in the past tense)

Perhaps this mortal fear, in which everything, even a grain of rice stuck to the bottom of the pot, the squeak of a cork, etc., wants to give me the death blow, is only there to teach me control—and yet when that feebleminded couple were here a while ago and I felt obliged to give my full attention to listening to what they said and understanding what they are, my condition grew even worse. I had thought I could escape into the perception of others, and saw that that was just what made me sick

And yet I fought against death all day, quietly, attentively, craftily

The President of the Republic is so intimidated on TV that his face actually takes on the lines of the popular caricatures; sometimes before saying a word he makes false mouth movements in the void, until at last he gets the beginning of the word right (the President will never accept the thought of Frenchmen firing on Frenchmen)

Thought: If I, instead of all those other people, had seen a flying saucer, it might have saved me

When the TV goes off at about midnight, I am in danger again (I had started laughing at the jokes again)

At the worst moment I wanted to buy newspapers, to pretend to be living a normal day

To stand up and walk—happiness!

Still stirrings and twinges of pain in my bones despite my almost anesthetic drunkenness

My inability to accept help from anyone—that, too, is a kind of coldheartedness, of indifference

This man who is now undressing is still I

Someone phoned, wants to come and see me tomorrow; I foolishly told him to press the bell a long time

March 25

Woke up in the dark. Panic. Slipped on a coat over my pajamas and went out into the street; a bird is piping; sounds like a man calling his dog (5 a.m.)

The small narrow world of a frightened man

I walked rapidly through the streets. A bus passed and I could make out passengers in the dark; the inside of the bus wasn't lit yet

Subject myself to *other* pain than salvation

Cats on garbage heaps

From a cellar the roar of a furnace

Not many lights on; those mostly in attic rooms

Wet bundles of newspapers by the lighted but deserted bus stops

Clouds of smoke from a chimney, though it's still deep night

Suddenly, though there were very few cars, the feeling that all hell had broken loose (panic)

Rain on my eyeballs, cool and soothing

While giving a blood sample, the shadow of drops of blood

The rustling of paper beside a sick man

At last, after long perplexity, I succeeded in catching my thoughts (write down every trifle at once—to find out what calmed me)

A little while ago (evening), for the first time in ever so long —while standing at the kitchen sink eating grapes and spitting the seeds into my hand—I managed to think of a future

March 26

They laid me down on a blanket and folded it over me

Lying feet foremost in the ambulance, in a traffic jam on the freeway. The sun was very hot and there was no need for me to be lying down; they made me

In the hospital. When I asked the doctor if I could go home the next day, she said: "It's within the realm of possibility"

I've started talking to myself again, if only inwardly. Good sign?

All the people here tell the doctor their stories, and she claims to know life in all its aspects; yet one has the feeling that she knows it in only the one aspect that's accessible to her as a doctor

While reading *Beneath the Wheel*: through writing give to the young the dignity that life has denied them

The one moment of silence during my roommate's wife's visit occurs when in taking leave she kisses her sick husband on both cheeks—or rather, a moment later

March 27

The power of tenderness, which suddenly dissolved the resistance that constituted my ego

The doctor asked the elderly patient (three heart attacks) when he was born, and when he said August, she burst into a subdued sanctimonious ecstasy: "Oh, that's vacation time." I noticed that regardless of the patient's history she always had the same questions and remarks in readiness: they should look within themselves for the cause of their illness, she had often had the same experience, etc. The look on her face when she was with us was so beamingly far away. Sometimes when she seemed a picture of sympathy and attentiveness, she would ask the same question all over again; she had forgotten not only the answer but her own question as well! Gestures and facial expression indicating total presence when she was miles away. (I'd like to encounter this woman at least once more in my life, for my "private pleasure.") —She came in a moment ago and said with a reassuring wave of the hand: "Keep calm! Don't make mountains out of molehills! Don't get stuck in the tunnel!" (And her replacement gives one the same long, empty look)

I sensed that the doctor would want to shake hands with me before she left, so I held my hands in the draft to keep them from sweating

One night there was something thrashing around under me, as if it were in the mattress; I thought I was dreaming, but I wasn't sure, so I moved to another bed, and there again something was thrashing around, some wild imprisoned thing in a paroxysm of claustrophobia—and two days later I found a dying rat breathing faintly on the red linoleum in the kitchen; I swept it into the dustpan and slid it into a plastic bag; then I carried the bag down to the courtyard and put it in the garbage

Doctors are always saying "a little," "just a little": "Did you spit a little blood again?" "Your blood pressure has gone up just a little"

All these unknown people, all these busy sounds—they really do comfort me "a little"

Or they use euphemisms like: "Of course a medical examination isn't exactly a picnic . . ." and tautologies like: *"L'hôpital c'est l'hôpital"*

To feel master of myself and my body again: how marvelous!

The sudden thought that if the oppressive feeling in my chest went away, my feeling of being alive would go away, too

Since his third heart attack the old man has been accompanying everything he says, even his jokes, with a resigned drooping of his arms or hands

Fear of death: you lose all feeling for the things you see, because your sense of humor is gone

Killed by orthodox reality

The moment the doctor said I had to go back to intensive care, the other patient put the newspaper I had lent him back on my bedside table

I'm almost looking forward to having another blood sample taken

The blinker light on the electrocardiograph and the blinker lights of the planes coming in for a landing, outside the window

March 28

I keep frantically cleaning my fingernails

The *Alarme* button of the electrocardiograph flickers as if it were going to light up; the *Seuil* button has stopped blinking and just keeps flickering. It's Sunday, and I've set my watch an hour ahead for summertime. I'm alone with the machine

It comforts me to have the vacuum cleaner with the long hose moving around me and the mop being pushed over the PVC flooring; the pleasant smell of ammonia. The squishy mop and the wheezing cleaning woman make almost the same sound (an indication that for moments at least I've recovered a bit of humor); now I've got back the word for the sound of the mop: it *wheezes*, like the woman who's pushing it

It's been light for quite some time, planes have been roaring past for hours. Condensation is dripping down the inside of the mineral water bottle, the flowers have been given fresh water, the sun has been shining into the room for ever so long—but it seems to me that the night is just ending

During the night a woman kept letting out short screams in the corridor (or maybe it was the squeaky wheels of a bed being moved): someone weeping and dying

If everyone knew how absolutely weird and far out he was, if everyone realized that he maintains his normalcy only by an unbroken series of carefully hidden tricks, he would be unable to do harm to others (this idea came to me while thinking about a man who has a compulsion to step outside for a moment once every day, there to experience a totally unmotivated terror, which he *needs*, but which he disavows on all other occasions and even ridicules in others)

The other patients cough at least, they have something else the matter with them

The screaming woman during the night: her short, utterly frantic screams seemed to issue from a *thing*; as though in her deadly panic she no longer dared to scream; a little like the howling of a dog when someone steps on his paw, but incessant

Last night in a dream I saw a tree lit by the first sun (as though sprinkled with light)—so intense, as I slept, was my longing for day

Maybe the screams during the night were only someone laughing and gasping for air

I've begun to see an electrocardiogram even in the scratches on the wall (which must have been made by a bed rubbing against it; the plaster has been scraped off in jagged zigzags)

Oddly enough, it makes me uneasy to think that my state of thoughtlessness may soon return, and when I hear a passing train I am dismayed at the thought that I may soon have to sit in such a train day after day: presentiment of unconsciousness and above all of emptiness

Just before the nurses go off duty, they are so flurried they start introducing all their sentences with *"Bon . . ."* (the doctor also says *"bon"* a lot when preparing to leave a patient)

Instead of moving to get warm, I do it by sitting absolutely motionless and trying to think

As the young doctors out in the observation room were looking at my electrocardiogram, the nurse stood up and began to sing; her purpose, I feared, was to shut the door to my room without my noticing, so I wouldn't hear what the doctors were saying

"Relax!" (But how?)

Looking out the window, I am surprised at the sight of something perfectly commonplace, a plane coming in for a landing in the sunlight (the plane *appears*)

What do I do in my moment of panic? I raise my hand and straighten my glasses

Even in my handwriting I've come to see an electrocardiogram

Brown drops on the wall. They seem to have been sprayed on from below, because the higher ones are lighter in color; they start at the bottom with a long fine line and look like drop-shaped parachutes with point-shaped jumpers attached; in another place a blue liquid has run in worm shapes

Sometimes the consciousness of death strikes me as a bet (though I couldn't say whom I was betting with) and as such amuses me in a way

The West Indian who hands out bread before meals has shed his skin twice a year since he's been in Europe

With all this peace and quiet, this drowsiness in the afternoon, I have a feeling that someone is lurking somewhere like a spider: ready to rush to my aid

The patient who was just brought into intensive care is squeezing blue handkerchiefs in both fists

"Ne respirez plus, monsieur!"

An hour immobilized by fear

If I were to say out loud: "I don't want to die," I myself would be to blame for the phrases people would use in reply

The wasted out-of-doors!

The old man, helpless against the sadness of parting, pinched himself furiously in the leg when he saw his wife in tears, looking in at him through the little window

Now I feel really sick, but only with the fear that's been put into me here

He's an Armenian but says he feels French, because he fought in the French army

Headline in the paper: Twenty-year-old dies of heart attack. Relieved to see it was a horse

The airplane taking off, reflected in the electrocardiograph screen

Closing my eyes brings sudden relief (I had long been afraid to close them); in closing my eyes, I feel that I'm making a connection between my thoughts and my feelings, which are miles apart when my eyes are open

For the first time since I've been here, I feel a breath of the real out-of-doors day on my feet

Because of the fear they've instilled in me here, they will find in my blood just the thing that will show they had a right to instill fear in me

I need something I can read *word for word*—none of those sentences one recognizes at a glance and skips, as is almost always the case with newspapers and, sad to say, with most books. Craving for *The Elective Affinities*

How can sedatives help when my restlessness is rational, when it comes from my thoughts?

My needs (eating, drinking, etc.) have become so unreal that, though aware of them, I keep putting them off until I forget them

Even in writing the worst of horrors, I often catch myself grinning. Therein lies the humor of awareness, of perception; to lose this humor—that would be a psychological catastrophe

Words as instruments of murder: "daybreak," "sunset," "the hour of the wolf," *"entre chien et loup"* . . .

I shut my eyes, but fear opens them

In saying: "Imagine myself as a corpse," I lifted my chin at the last word, as though uttering words of defiance

New-found happiness: being able to look at a bottle of mineral water (that wonderful feeling: there *is* something else!)

Convinced that I must forget the past entirely if I am to re-cover from this pain in my chest: *I must lose my memory!* In opposition to the sheltered bourgeois consciousness with its love of memory and remembered view of itself (my battle against the memory that has hemmed me in since childhood: memory threatens me with death!)

How unlovingly the young girl who used to give me such languishing looks stared at me in the hospital room!

Thought: If there were a God, then only for someone else; for me, *as I am now,* there is no God

I hear the dog barking outside in the evening; I *am able* to listen! (Happiness)

I don't feel at home in illness (as so many others do)

This afternoon I was in such a state I came close to asking the most despised of humankind to help me

March 29

A train at daybreak—: the sound seems to issue from the rising dawn; and then the distant roar of the train, the rattling of individual cars, and for a moment a little squeaking sound; how beautiful the dawn is today; for a few moments the train rattles as though crossing a small bridge

Now that I've got through the night it's almost beautiful to hear my roommate's snoring and the gurgling in his belly

If I count my heartbeats more slowly than they occur, they *become* slower

The young nurse gives me a violent rubdown for fear the movement of her hands on my back will feel like a caress

I become an empty *cavern* when the tension of my fear goes out of me

The vague shadows of flowers on the sunlit fever chart; they are more beautiful than the real flowers in the window; shadow forms, surrounded by a second wreath of much fainter shadows or designs, like a ring of mold growing out of the central shadow; the flowers are so far away from the paper on which they cast their shadows that the shadows have no clear outlines; only the blossoms cast shadows, not the stems, so that the shadows of these blossoms hover in mid-air; what makes these designs seem more beautiful than the real flowers is their unconnectedness; losing their reality, these hospital flowers become shadow, while at the same time a new, unknown form is created

At the sight of the sunlit tree trunks outside, a warmth gradually rises up in me that connects me with the outside

Someone who cries with his eyes closed like the old man next to me can have no fear of death; he is only grieved at the thought that perhaps he will never again be with those he loves

The kindness of sufferers from heart disease (a precaution?)

The sound of my roommate's electric shaver submerges my perception of myself; I am afraid (that was my only reason for picking up the glass of water and putting it down again)

Against my will I told my story again

"You are entitled to one gram of salt a day!" And the nurse shook the little packet in front of the patient, as though she thought he had lost his power to understand the spoken language

The blowing forsythia outside—there's something important inside it; I close my eyes to find out what it is—and suddenly I feel the yellow imprint of the blossoms on my face! My face goes so deep into the writhing yellow bush that there is more yellow than I can take in, a soft, exclusive, but utterly motionless yellow, beneath the restlessly billowing surface; as though this totally immobile yellow center in the landscape were something *for me, apart from me*; as though the real yellow began only under the swaying branches

Happiness: I can still reach for a book

Once again: I must lose my memory. I must lose *my* memory and become a memory for others

Now I try to make out the tune when someone whistles in the corridor

He looked into my eyes as only a very sick man can look into one's eyes

The electrodes cling almost lovingly to my chest

Far away in the cemetery, many light-colored tombstones in the sun; a man in gray is walking among them and his motion seems very rapid among the stones, which are as big as he is; though in fact he is moving slowly from tombstone to tombstone, the light-colored, closely spaced stones flicker like a stroboscope as he passes

In reading Kafka's *Diaries*, I find that his complaints and self-recriminations no longer interest me, but only his descriptions

In the two months of his stay here the old man has begun to act like a schoolboy; for instance, he raises both hands when asked if he wants bread and answers in the croaking voice of a first-grader

Reading Kafka: no need to remember his actual words (you can forget them right away, that's the fine thing about them); they remain present all the same, even if you forget them

The fear I've again begun to feel is just my everyday fear— the only difference is that the setting now is a hospital

While I was reading a book, the old man in the other bed was reading the label on a mineral-water bottle, turning the bottle around and around

"What's so funny about this thing you're telling me?" — "It's funny because I'm able to tell you about it"

Idea of death: a big apple that you hold by the stem; you hold it still for a long long time, until you discover what weight is

The image of rolling pebbles on the bottom of a clear brook, and in my head the words: "The minds of the dead roll with the pebbles in the brook"

("I should have to search for a year to find a true feeling inside me"—K.)

What I refuse to put up with: people referring to me as "he" in my presence

The vocabulary of hospital visitors' French: sorry to say, I understand every word of it

The sick man asked his wife what time it was; she didn't tell him the time but only said: "Fifteen minutes" (meaning she would have to leave in fifteen minutes)

Something that weighed on me for many years: once when I was a child, a fortune-teller told my mother that I would be a civil servant!

The moment M. stepped into the sickroom, it was *her* room; whereas G. just hung around like a stranger the whole time, getting in everyone's way

At last, night is falling; two patients sit silently side by side in their beds, both intermittently scratching and jiggling and fidgeting

A way to calm myself: write letters or numbers in such a way that feeling and hand remain one (the feeling should not rush ahead before the hand writes)

The old man wants his slippers put down at his bedside "in the right direction," so he can step right into them

"Doctors are stupid, or, rather, they are no stupider than anyone else, but their pretensions are ridiculous, yes indeed, once you start dealing with them, you can only expect them to get stupider and stupider . . ." (to Milena)

March 30

I've already begun to think: We invalids

Last night the old man beside me sighed and groaned, loudly and pitifully as if he were dying—actually, as he told me in the morning, he hadn't even been in pain, it was only the strange sensation of urinating through a catheter

Instead of getting lighter as the day dawns, the sky clouds over and gets darker and darker

In the bright room the shadows of birds darting by

When the old man asks a question, the nurse answers by repeating his question in a slight singsong. The patient: "Is the tube fastened?"—The nurse (in a singsong): "The tube is fas-tened"

He calls out something to the nurse as she is leaving, but she doesn't hear him; the cry that escapes him makes me think of a hunter who has missed his aim

Someone says something to someone else who doesn't hear it, but others in the room hear it—a few moments of paralyzed silence

Occasionally the long-time patient speaks to the nurses in an undertone, as if they had secrets together

The visitor told us about his sick relative: "He was the president of a firm, the *first* president of *his* firm." Just as a relative of mine, a saleswoman, used to say: "The bookkeeping is *under me.*" Or: "I am *in charge* of the food department" (which didn't amount to a row of pins). She also used to say that her young brother was "studying to be a *mechanical draftsman* and a machinist *at the same time.*" Her husband used to say: "I have an art gallery" (it was actually a craft shop). And once when I met a girl I had known in grade school she, too, was "directing an art gallery." When I asked about her father, he was *"on the staff of the highways department."* Then I remembered that he was a road worker, and had a vision of a man standing shovel in hand beside a pile of gravel—big-mouths ashamed of their littleness!

For once a nurse who speaks without exaggerating, who speaks as she feels (and as I like)

"The first anxiety of the day"

I'm beginning to see flowers as flowers (only yesterday this tulip looked to me like a head of cabbage)

The elderly patient is caressing the nurse's finger*nail*

The question used to be: How should I live? Now: How should I think? (But the same intense rhetoric)

My taking notes in front of them doesn't affect their behavior in the least (maybe a writer, like a policeman, should wear a uniform, so people can watch their step in his presence)

The old man says to himself: *Mon pauvre ami!*

The nurse accidentally stepped on the transparent bag in which the old man's urine had collected. It looked like a plastic bag of bloody supermarket meat that has been kept in the icebox for several days

Visiting me in the hospital, G. was as excited as I've only known him to be on the telephone, where for fear of missing something his heart pounds so that he catches practically nothing

When an idiot leaves the room, we don't talk about him, but resolve with a silent gesture to forget him

In knowledge I feel weaker than certain writers (Hesse, for instance); in poetic penetration of the world, stronger

The head physician of the section comes in and dangles his hand in front of me for me to shake (without looking at me); while listening to the old man, he faces away from him, and the old man has to talk up to his ear

I must get used to moving slowly for the rest of my life

The old man asked me: "These books you write—are they taken from life or out of the air?" — "Both," I said

I haven't had time to look out the window yet today

The old man is leaving the hospital; his hat is lying ready, with his wife's knitting beside it; all through his illness she has spent the visiting hours silently knitting at his bedside

Before being carted out in a wheelchair, the old man put on the wide gray-on-gray checked loden coat he bought more than twenty years ago in a shop that no longer exists; his plastic bag, half full of urine, hung down below his coat. With tears in his eyes, he waved goodbye to me, then they wheeled him out to the elevator; when he got home, he'd go to bed and sleep

Suppose I had to write a story that would not seem absurd to someone tied hand and foot, gagged, and shut up in a clothes cupboard

New colors in the room: the patient they've just brought in has a rust-brown operation scar on his chest, and there's a greenish-yellow sachet of lavender on top of his pile of linen

Barely settled, he's busy marking the menu for a whole week ahead

My first fear of the day; not bad, it's already late afternoon; I must try to delay this fear a little longer each day!

I believe that my eyes lit up once today

As soon as I start feeling fairly well, I find it hard to look at people with sympathy, to feel for them, etc.

What would I do without the comings and goings of the planes outside! John Cowper Powys, sometimes the machines you curse *are* of some use to a man's soul

Years of pain have taught the new patient in my room to lie as still as a mouse; he never turns over in bed

The fact is that when I like myself (approve of myself, have a conception of myself) I get silly ideas about myself

My skin is still sticky where the electrodes were placed

March 31

I don't dare wish my roommate a good morning; maybe he's in pain

I smell the bread and I'm disappointed—as though a fool-proof system had failed to function

Gradually, as the day dawns, the bouquet shows its colors: the yellow first

I let my thoughts wander until I could feel myself

The bedridden man is beginning to confuse the shapes of things; in the thorns of roses, for example, he sees parrot beaks

Never *look* for metaphors! (They must be *experienced*)

My new roommate gives me the feeling that I've changed rooms

Fear of death had become acceptance of death

The patient beside me wants a haircut—never in all his life has his hair been so long

Strange how sick people lose all national characteristics

I'm already curious about my roommate's wife

Elegance as a quality in a woman rather than an attitude—I like that

This patient breathes as if he were blowing into an empty bottle

The cosmic-blue sky

Suppose that, after thinking all the possibilities through, I reverted to the lyrics of hit songs

Wanting to assault the flowers—with both hands

Smoke among the pines in the distance; their trunks are very dark in contrast to the light-colored trunks of the deciduous trees; it's so lovely outside, so all-pervadingly peaceful; the smoke makes the pines look even darker; the long hedge shines as if it alone were wet in the whole still, sunny landscape; even the flashing hoods of the cars emanate a kind of American peace; in the fork of a tree a tiny piece of silver paper flashes stupendously; the freshly sawed branch stumps shine as if that were the only thing to do—all so fearless that even the birds go strolling about on the ground, in the grass, instead of flying (fable of the bird who wished it could walk on the earth, just as men long to fly). And suddenly, looking out on this paradisiacal landscape, I think: *rockslide*

"Yes, my friend, I'll lend you the money—but then it's all over between us and I don't want anything more to do with you"

One of the few gestures in *The Elective Affinities*: ". . . said Eduard, rubbing his forehead"

"You women," said Eduard, "would be irresistible if you were like this: so wise that one cannot contradict you, so loving that one gladly gives in to you, so sensitive that one would not wish to wound you, so full of forebodings that one is terrified"

At last I laughed myself back to the surface of the earth

Lying there with my eyes closed, I deliberately thrust out my lower lip, so as not to look like a corpse in my own mind

The world that grows on to one's heart

A man has been lying beside me for a whole day, and I've just now noticed that he has only one arm

He isn't in utter despair yet, he hasn't begun to be thankful

The landscape outside: soothing beauty; not, however, as though the revelation were already at hand, but as though it were imminent—as though it were imminent and would remain so forever

The people in the sunlight are walking so slowly that they invariably put down one foot after the other

Suddenly, as I doze, a sensation as if a cat had jumped up on the bed

Supposing that after all the usual years of petting and fondling, a real friendship were suddenly to spring up and the petting and fondling were no longer conceivable, no longer tolerable or necessary

"Aptitudes are assumed; we want them to develop into skills" (an examiner to Ottilie): there you have the essence of modern technocratic brutality (as though we had grown incapable of understanding Goethe's simplicity)

Ottilie: "A pleasant motion that goes on forever"

On the other hand, a man's soul can't feed forever on the sight of a bush glittering in the evening wind

A twitching in the scar on the sleeper's shoulder, where there had been an arm before

The world becomes describable—at last a feeling is connected with an object (epic writing)

When the man is in pain, his eyes open and close involuntarily

". . . he grasped her hand and pressed it to his eyes. These perhaps were the most beautiful hands that had ever been joined"

From a book review: "This is more than a piece of great literature." *What* is more than a piece of great literature?

The sick man hasn't even the strength to clear his throat

I was asleep, and when I opened my eyes I saw first the green and red felt-tipped pens she had promised me on her visit the day before; then her hand and then her hair (moment of love)

"Some clumsy new servants were wearing the livery": a picture of bad times in general, not only of the nineteenth century

While watching a football game on TV: never again will I let my obsession with death stop me from looking at fine things

What a loss if I hadn't seen that commercial on TV! (My affection for commercial images, their familiar omnipresence, insouciance, contempt for death)

Maybe the illumination is always with me, and I should just make an effort to take it in

". . . paltry comfort that even sorrows such as this are appeased by time. She cursed the time it takes to appease them; she cursed the deathlike time when they would be appeased." As I reexperience these old sentences, I hear a train outside in the night, and in the very moment of being heard, the train seems to be outlived by the sentences: it's not the sentences that are anachronistic, but this train that has burst in on them. "They spent part of the night talking and joking about many things, all the more freely because, sad to say, the heart had no part in it." — " 'You love me,' he cried. 'Ottilie, you love me.' And they held each other entwined. No one could have said which of them had first clasped the other"

Moments when everything individual, cross-grained, ego-touting is so appeased by active happiness and at the same time by pain (the one conditions the other), and when this so expands me, so frees me from limits, that I truly feel a kind of *world* soul rather than my own restricted one

April 1

A long stay in one place seems to make for anthropomorphic vision—and this anthropomorphic vision of the sick, or of prisoners, in any case of persons confined for a long time to a single place, would seem to be another possible reality and by no means (as Robbe-Grillet has decreed) a literary cliché; as a mode of perception rooted in my own situation, it would thus go far beyond such sentences as "The village nestled in the valley"; and one fine morning, there would be nothing to prevent a long-stemmed rose against the morning sky from looking proud—to me, for instance, after prolonged nightmares ("After confused humiliating nightmares I beheld, at the moment of waking, the outline of a self-assured long-stemmed rose against the gray dawning sky")

Just now for the first time I saw an airplane flying in a different direction from the one they usually fly here—suddenly a faint intimation of war

The fading tulip smells like dandelions

My (to myself irksome) faculty of "seeing through" people—hence, my frequent listlessness in company

"He wanders about, he is the most restless and the happiest of mortals. He strolls through the gardens; they are too small for him; he rushes into the fields, they are too spacious." "Eduard's opinions as well as his actions have thrown aside all measure. The knowledge that he loves and is loved drives him to the infinite." — "He tried to help himself by a kind of humor which, however, since it was without love, lacked the usual charm" (as in *Indian Summer*, the patience needed for reading is not given in advance; it is produced by reading)

Here in the hospital I ceased for a time to be anything else but "my condition," "my situation," "my circumstances"

The barber in the sickroom, the bunches of hair on the sickroom floor ("I couldn't sleep with all that hair," said the patient who has now become a customer—of the barber)

Dismissed from the hospital on this most beautiful day of all possible days, I cannot dispel the feeling (?) that I wouldn't be missing anything if I were dead

"Outside," in the city, I discover who I am, who I have become

Today I have to sit down to get back in rhythm with the world (usually I do it by walking)

A new season: the park paths are once again strewn with those little sticks of wood that Eskimo pies are attached to

A feeling of inferiority when I see faces without yearning

Elegance: getting out of the way gracefully

When I jot something down while standing, I feel like a policeman writing out parking tickets

In this pure light the houses seem to consist entirely of sparkling façades

Suddenly such a feeling of happiness that each one of my bodily functions, which can be bothersome at other times, becomes a part of it

Strange: I couldn't bear it any longer among the young, exuberant, airy, cheerful people on the boulevard—I feel so much happier here in the park among older, wearier people, women with poodles sitting on rusty green chairs, children

I can see myself writing like this forever, as far as the center of the world

A woman turns away when I look at her (a mere act of perception). For a moment I feel like saying: "I'm really not doing you any harm"

On this warm afternoon the women are coming out of the office buildings in coats (it was cold this morning), and I can hear them all sigh with relief; no, there are some who no longer even sigh with relief when they come out of their offices into this beauty

Shaken by the Métro again, along with everyone else

At the sight of the switchblade, the thought that I could use it to defend myself if my own body assaulted me

April 2

The call of a blackbird in a tall poplar: seems unusually loud

Closed eyes: they make me think of the Veronica

Back to normal: looking through all my pockets for change again

A new idiocy, the following sentence by a writer: "We must ask these academics: How could they stay home that day when the Americans, in defiance of all agreements, unleashed their bombs and napalm on Cambodia? What did they do that day?" (The mystique of "staying home" and "taking-it-to-the-streets": as though staying home could only mean indifference, and taking-it-to-the-streets were a positive guarantee of grief and rage)

The face of an actor with a jutting lower lip: a face that seems to say: This man would never listen to me, and I'd have nothing to say to him anyway (and yet this same face was capable of trembling when the actor played the part of a dying man)

Strange emotion when I read: *"Dans un terrain vague"* (a dead child was found)

Crowd outside a shop window where a computer is issuing horoscopes for the next five years: I notice that, as a spectator "above this kind of thing," I was going to raise my eyebrows —but then I just watch

G. said that thus far he had experienced the fear of death only for seconds at a time; that he couldn't bear it any longer

Once the moment of horror is past—I think I am (or was) exaggerating

April 3

Sitting after a long walk: a pleasure to watch the passing women

The half-sleep images I get when inside my closed eyes I am able to close my eyes again: then even the stones come to life

Things I notice: things to take home with me

Half-sleep image of a man whose head was all covered with mice and glittered in the sun

"I wanted to tell you that I have become really fond of you." At these words something happened in my penis, not excitement, only a perception, a taking-notice: "Perception is attention" (Novalis)

Shortly before she wakes, the child's sleep changes; though she is still in a deep sleep, sounds emerge through her still silent breathing, as though she were gathering the strength to wake up: a sigh, a loud yawn, a humming, but all still immersed in deep sleep; then lip sounds, smacking, popping, and above all slight breathing sounds, whereas during the night the only sounds were dream conversations or teeth-gnashing

Half-sleep images—the more beautiful they are, the more terrifying, for in their beauty, even if they show me nothing more than flowers in a rolling meadow, they emanate death rays that fasten on to me; sacred groves (which may be nothing more than gravel paths in a park) dart their rays at me, and I wake up in a panic, fearing to be sucked into them, into a fervent, glittering, bucolic nothingness in which I will lose both body and soul. These miraculous, archaic, divine, sublime, vast, triumphantly silent images, which unite near and far, are my first experiences of nothingness, which hitherto has been only an unlived word for me

When A. wakes up and sees me writing again, she smiles

Idea: when, at last, will a dead person succeed in really coming back, in being here again? It must be possible

I've already had a few moments today of feeling benevolent toward the sunny world

"You don't like to move the camera much, do you?" — "No, because it throws the audience off. It says: 'This is a motion picture. This isn't real.' I like to have the audience feel that this is the real thing" (John Ford, 1970)

One thing that having money has taught me: to hold out my hand and wait imperturbably until *all* the change has been given

Walking, the inner cry: Ah, at last I'm alive again! And the pleasant prospect of being able to go straight to my destination

Attract attention by imperceptibility (not allow anyone to look at me)

Sometimes my associations, involuntary confusion of one thing with another, etc., get on my nerves; there seems to be something professional about this involuntariness—as if I were responsible even for my reflexes

A little dog was being dragged over the sidewalk; his nails scratched audibly against the cement, because he didn't move his legs, just let himself be dragged

Sometimes, after several successive mishaps, I talk to myself (it helps)

And then again the thought that everything I think and feel is irrelevant

An unhappy woman with a child clinging to her sat opposite me. I was prepared to give her the friendliest look imaginable, it might have helped her—but she didn't do me the favor of looking at me

When Frau F. is feeling out of sorts, she pulls the sleeves of her sweater over her fists

Two lovers met halfway between the cities where they lived. They sat silently in the park of the unfamiliar town, and when at last she called his attention to two poodles, he was very sad, disillusioned at her being able to notice anything else but him

How she discovered that he meant something to her: There was a tassel attached to the zipper of his knitted vest, and once when he was visiting her at her parents' house he tore it off and dropped it or threw it away. Later, when she found the tassel on the floor, she suddenly realized that the two of them were made for each other

Sometimes people from whom one expected nothing at all are full of the most amazing stories. But how is one to get their stories out of them without making them feel that they have been robbed of their secrets?

"How often does your sadness grip your very throat?" writes Herr F. in one of his poems

Sometimes in the evening they go out on the balcony and close the door, just for the pleasure of looking in at their big lighted apartment

April 4

Why do I never fall asleep until I know it's the next day!

The bullfight in Valencia: the mortally wounded bull did not collapse *in front of* the torero, but took a few steps *to one side,* turned away from the man who had killed him, and fell onto the sand; I could hardly hold back the tears

Someone asked me what I was thinking just then, and I didn't know; that gave me the feeling that, as far as he was concerned, my conscience was clear

Perhaps in the last moment of life, for dignity's sake, I will clasp my knees to my belly as the people of Pompeii did when Vesuvius erupted

A moment of kindness, of contentment, of open sky in a cold, drizzling, disgruntled day with the television sounds pouring from a dozen windows, though the afternoon has hardly begun

People whispering in a waiting train

A.'s dream: a dog with two mouths—one wide open, the other closed—was looking at her

Alone in the big, rattling, creaking elevator to the observation tower: and then the view through glass to the tree-lined streets far below; not so long ago I was wandering about in those same streets in the early dawn, with my fear

When I'm in this state, a lot of people try to give me warmth, but I don't seem capable of taking it in (a day with cut-off eyelids)

View through a window into someone's home. Grownups and children. Outside, the twilight; inside, lamps already lit. The feeling that these grownups and these children had their souls taken away long ago and are sitting there alone in a hopeless, boundless grief, which crushes me, too

Those people over there are just noisy card players. And already I catch myself thinking: not for me

With this panorama before me I lost my sense of humor once again, and my fear prevented me from recognizing anything

April 5

In suit and overcoat I dived for a sunken city; I didn't find it, but when I came up I lied and said I had seen it

My feeling of manginess vis-à-vis society

The moment I set foot in the house, there was a vague friendly smell. When I entered the apartment, it identified itself with the owner's bedtime pipe

In the park. Wanting to sit on a metal chair rather than on the wooden bench—seems safer

Gazing into space, looking for something to hold me steady

Perhaps if someone were actively unkind to me now, I would become more real

Even on a beautiful day like this the underground passages of the Métro are full of people and there are lines waiting to get into the movie houses

Maybe my feeling of unreality, of unconnectedness, comes from all the mint and linden-blossom tea I've got into the habit of drinking every day

An almost fearless evening, rich in forbearance

When they all started telling jokes, I realized that I hardly knew any; I was delighted

April 6

When B. is drunk he doesn't wait, as usual, until he feels what he is going to say and has thought it over; his contagious thoughtfulness goes overboard and he chatters; he keeps taking back what he has said, but goes right on with his chatter

"Maybe," she said, "some women's elegance is a defense mechanism"

The plane trees outside the café—the dangling seed pods are there again

After spring vacation: certain mothers look feebleminded with their suntan

Sometimes the fresh green leaves are clothed in light; our bodies, too, are held fast in it, and we are quietly contented; the campuslike quality of certain blue-green springtime hours, their carefree, provisional quality; without engaging in any particular sport, I feel like a sportsman

Sometimes a feeling of well-being takes hold of me—as though a hand were gently closing inside my body

Softly clearing my throat out of fear

And then again carefree moments, when the sun widens my lips, gives me honest-to-goodness lips

As if to congratulate me, Frau F. goes on pumping my hand much longer than there's any reason to; you'd think she was doing it for the photographers

Although her husband had sent her to buy just one thing in a hurry, I saw her stop in spite of herself to look into shop windows; out on the street, among strangers, her face had become sullen and thin-lipped, and she looked very small to me

After starting to drink, I became curious (though there was nothing in particular that I wanted to know)

April 7

A small fear, I decided, was unworthy of my attention. Instantly I was plunged in unreality and my fear became gigantic

I wish I could be more often as I was yesterday (saying and doing only what I wanted to and felt like); when that happens I don't wake up the day after with my head full of painful sentences or gestures produced without feeling

Since I put on the record ("I know you're dying, baby, and I know you know it, too") the sky has turned blue and clouded over again, showing that Van Morrison was right

The expression of a person who is very much loved and finds it hard to bear, but tries to understand that the other is in the right

All the things that do not interest me but that I am nevertheless forced to notice are trying to kill me

More and more people are "taken" when I want them (like seats at the movies)

The feeling that I have only *one* big eye; in my fear everything seems fused into one and projected outward

In a railroad compartment with folding seats along the walls, jiggling straps, and no place to sit down—this is where I belong now

In the mirror the reflection of nostrils dilated with the will to live

It's starting to rain. As though someone were throwing a pebble now and then

"Wide as he opened his eyes, no world went in and out"

Snuggling up to a cushion in the storeroom

Living images: ". . . I thought I was in another world; except that the presence of reality, instead of making for illusion, gave me a feeling of anxiety"

Images from the past that crash in my head like planes out of a clear sky

"Nothing in the world seemed incoherent to her when she thought of the man she loved . . ."

I wanted to look serene in the photo, but the person I saw in it was morose

A brief pain, followed by long thinking games (until the next brief pain)

At the crucial moment I managed to make her afraid of me—in that way I avoided (for both of us) the calamity of her love

April 8

Last night, suddenly waking from a dream, I saw the worm that had been responsible for my dream, as though I had cut into the bark of a tree and surprised a noxious grub

Every thought of something that *must* be done, even the most trifling action, such as changing one's shirt, seems confining

At the movies. I try to divert my panic to the seat in front of me

No questions, please, no questions!

I wonder how many other people—those, for instance, whom I disposed of as "vain" in the course of the day—run their hands over their hair, as I'm doing now, for no other reason than because they are in a panic

All at once I understood why at the last moment the dying "turn toward the wall" (the bull going off to one side)

The girl looked at me and for a moment, defenseless with sympathy, I had the feeling that a coldhearted vulture was looking at me through her eyes

The quiet, imperceptible storm of time in my head—but occasionally a fragment goes astray, and then I perceive it

An evening without fear, when my heart beats deep down in my chest

April 9

They no longer criticize his way of acting, they criticize his whole being; in other words, he has achieved perfection as an actor

A woman who speaks fast and fluently on the phone, as though playing back a tape, taking account in advance of everything I might possibly say

I spin a top without thinking and forget about it; a few minutes later I look, and it's still quietly spinning

For some time now my anxiety has been so constant that I barely notice the usual petty terrors (a lens falling out of my glasses, etc.)

Wonderful moment late this afternoon when I was walking with A. Her chocolate bar, still with the silver paper around it, slipped out of the wrapper and fell to the street: the flash of the silver paper in the low-lying sun was the flare-up of a memory: my own chocolate bar slipping out of its wrapper long years ago. The moment was so comforting that my anger at the child's clumsiness was gone before it had time to erupt

D. is never ashamed of his dejection in company, never tries to conceal it, but sits there in heavy, obstructive silence, imposing it as his way of being himself—whereas I, in company, usually lose (and it really is a loss) my dejection, the visible expression of my dejection, and what's left of me is a nondescript, shapeless something, because my only feeling is one of dejection, which, however, I cease to feel in the company of others; I become absentminded for lack of feeling

When I told Herr F. about my crises, he said: "You've had a narrow escape." Then he told me how he played bicycle racer as a child; there was a curve with moss on it that was usually wet—and when he'd got around it without falling, but had come close to falling, he always said to himself proudly: "I sure had a narrow escape that time"

The formal element: not a finished product, but an activity

Paradisiacal moment: everything seems to be in its place, the houses in the sun, the pedestrians, the light-green leaves, the blue sky behind the leaves, a shutter opens, a bird sings, a hammer strikes: one thing after another, not concurrently or intermingled, that is what might be called paradisiacal; festive clarity (without the feast day) instead of the everyday blur

The child's slightly averted cheek: I am literally overwhelmed by the child's loneliness; how good-natured she is in her loneliness, how awkward in her loneliness

Faces that can take on a spark of life only in the moment of death

I noticed my inclination to pay with the shabby old bank notes rather than the new ones

Just to be able to say, as I do now: "I'm in a good humor"

Suddenly, when fear had at last occupied my whole body from top to toe, I was free from it (I had made slight attempts to dodge with the upper part of my body)

April 11

I wait impatiently for involuntary thoughts—those are the only ones that count

Fearing she would kill me with her oppressive, invasive love, which was really a desire to absorb me, I asked her if she would like to commit suicide; a bad joke in self-defense

Maybe the light-green trees are manifestations of the morning sun, made by the morning sun

The row of poplars is so dense that I sense the river behind them

After putting aside the newspapers with all their real happenings, I look around me and take a breath; then at last I am open to "what has really happened"

Child's voice on Sunday morning from one of the many open windows: "Mommy, where are my underpants?"

A poodle walking backward

The bourgeois couple step solemnly out of their house

The boss says he is very much disappointed in his employee (bosses are so often disappointed!)

April 12

For the first time in my life I've just seen a completely rusted television antenna. Joy!

Perhaps if a woman were really beautiful, beautiful without anxiety or effort, one would not have to sneak glances at her as one does with those who *try* to be beautiful; one could look at her openly, frankly moved, with curiosity, admiration, surprise, affection—and she would understand

There were more windows open on the cardiac floor than on any other floor of the hospital

Touch those flowers standing in the hot sun—they are so cool

Always trying to drum the "lessons of history" into us to teach us humanity—as if I couldn't find out what to do and what not to do just as well (or rather, a good deal better) without history

Be prepared to thrust aside a pistol barrel at any moment

On the plane trees, last year's big brown seedpods side by side with the small fresh green ones that give off dust when I touch them and smell of damp moss in my hand—and then, in the heart of the city, I see a sunken lane (not *mine*)

A woman gives me a hostile look and I look calmly back; then I notice that nothing has changed and forget the woman, hostility and all

There is really no solution, the eternal cleavage between me and the world remains, and the hope of overcoming it once and for all—by holding my breath in a certain way, for instance—is no better than an injection of some placebo; once in a while it works, though

French people always seem to be fighting—but then, in the midst of all the screaming and yelling, you see them grinning at each other

Reflex: whenever I see an elderly Frenchman in a business suit, I look at his buttonhole to see if he's wearing the rosette of the Legion of Honor

More and more quiet moments in the last few days; now I feel calm, anxiety seems quite impossible

April 13

The shoemaker in the gray smock hurries down the street on his way to work, opens the door to his shop without breaking his stride, and, full of dignity and determination, goes inside for the day

I've come to the point where I sometimes defend people who are being thoughtlessly attacked, instead of lapsing into a morose silence as I used to

An advertisement tells me that life is beautiful—a personal insult!

Bad writing: a betrayal

Old shoeprints in the asphalt: that was when pointed shoes were still in style! A hundred steps later, the rounded toes came along

One more literary idiocy: a woman writer, instead of showing that all psychoanalysis is invention, calls for the invention of a *female* psychoanalysis, made by women

As I laughed, it seemed to me that the light bulb flickered

The momentary thought that all life, even the tiniest vegetable organism, is a disease of the paradisiacally dead universe

Left-handed people often have ink smudges on the sides of their hands; in writing, they have to lift their hands off the paper to keep from blurring the letters

Full moon: now the moon is really here!

The complacency—another kind of armor—that comes of basking in thoughts that one has expressed successfully in the presence of others: such arrogance is directed against no one, but it impedes the constantly renewed perception without which there can be no life. Perhaps it's an affectation, a pretense, to express thoughts that don't arise *in the moment* of speaking

April 14

When some people talk, they stop whatever else they were doing (eating, dressing). A. is one of them

April chill in the schoolroom

The Eskimos regard anyone as "crazy" who talks to himself, shouts at someone who doesn't exist, refuses to talk, thinks he is an animal, runs away, hides in peculiar places, makes faces; the black Africans regard anyone as "crazy" who laughs when there's nothing to laugh at, talks uninterruptedly, throws food away for fear of poison, or imagines that his body gives off a perpetual odor

A., when accused of being greedy: "No, I'm not greedy—it's not *money* I want!"

"I love pressing buttons!" (Elevator, hall light, doorbell)

A child in conversation with a grownup—waiting for the grownup to make a fool of himself

"Are you angry with me?" — "Why?" — "Because you're walking so stooped over"

I actually succeed in getting through a moment of terror unruffled by simply continuing to breathe—but in the next moment a more insignificant object of terror provokes a doubly violent fear

The way American actors hold out their index fingers like revolvers in speaking; even the youngest of them are taking it up again

And with those compressed lips you think you're prepared for any woman who turns up!

"Do you know why my speaking voice is so high? — Because I used to sing. And *your* voice is high when you're tired"

Now, for the first time in ever so long, I can look on my body not as a phenomenon to be observed but with a kind of affection, a sense of solidarity

April 15

So tired that when I catch sight of myself in the mirror I'm surprised I still exist

"I always think of you" (the thought that someone is always thinking of me drives me crazy)

One moment of joy in the day: no thoughts

People passing me by, eyeless, forever

Maxim: "Act so that someone who knows you will recognize you if he runs into you on the street"

Suspicion that outbursts of rage make me older, or at least make me look older

A. doesn't say anything, but she is ashamed because of the way I scolded the people who pushed into the cab ahead of us; she asks me for my pen; while feeling so ashamed of me she wants *something in her hand* to play with or just to hold

How much pure rhetoric goes back and forth in even the most serene and natural relationship

It is hard not to lose patience with the trifling but long-drawn-out stories a child tells; but if you succeed, it makes for closeness (the difficulty of listening was the beginning of my painful imprisonment in myself)

Pleasant sensation: to *throw* something tenderly! (Not into someone's arms; but simply, while thinking of the person it belongs to, to throw an object tenderly into the distance)

Twilight silence, only distant television sounds; suddenly a bird fluttering in the bushes

Suddenly, in the little yard behind the tall building, a gust of wind in the shrubbery

Gradually the outward *stillness* of the evening becomes an inward bodily *warmth*

I'm sitting in the silent garden; inside the house, the child is lying in bed, turning the pages of a book

Drawing something a few days ago, I succeeded for the first time in making a sweeping line (up until then I had only made little jerky lines)

"She was happy when Eduard was near, and felt that she must now send him away" (*"And* felt"! Not "so that" or "consequently"!)

"I was neither asleep nor awake; I was dozing"

April 16

In the middle of the night A. patted *me*, because *she* had had a nightmare; "in the middle of the night she patted me; she had had a nightmare"

The water out of the tap is so cold; it must be a cold morning outside

Suddenly love sets in and I start running—up a flight of stairs

Look at a photograph and say to it: "Save me!" Then tear it up

A.'s dream: three arms grow out of a flowerpot and start carrying her away; she cuts the arms off with a pair of scissors, but they get longer and longer. When she woke up, she held her eyes open with her fingers, to keep from seeing the dream

The habit of calling a child by an epithet: "Greedy," "Forgetful," "Lazy," etc. (rather than by name)

Learn to control the impulse to rush to the rescue when a child is doing something difficult—not helping is itself a kind of help, a sign of sympathy; whereas the frantic impulse to help is often a mere defense against the more difficult acts of assistance that will be necessary later on

The danger of being delighted "too soon" and of being exhausted and indifferent at the decisive moment

The right kind of care: when, while busying myself with A., I still have eyes for something else, for instance, at the present moment, for the city beneath our plane; the kind of care that excludes everything else is compulsive and affected (I am sometimes guilty of it, I admit); to care for someone and at the same time keep one's eyes and ears open to other things strikes me as the right way, because then one can pass on one's perceptions as a kind of tranquilizer to the person being cared for

I stacked the dirty dishes as quietly as possible for fear of infecting anyone with the idea of helping me

He looked up from his magazine, saw the glow of the setting sun on the houses, and immediately put the magazine aside

On the way through the center of the city, the taxi driver, knowing me for an out-of-towner, has been pointing out all the sights. I'm looking forward to the suburbs, where there will be nothing to point out

Standing at dusk in the rain-drenched garden of a villa, armed with the insensibility of one who knows with certainty that his life will go on, and how . . .

April 17

Engage in activity until it becomes an occupation which can be called work and which satisfies me (something more than mere symbolic manipulations, such as putting one plate on top of another after breakfast)

Emptied the tea bag of camomile blossoms into the garbage. In that same moment a vision of open chicken gizzards, still full of corn kernels

Sometimes, in watching the simplest possible activity, e.g., someone cutting a piece of cloth, I feel absolutely incapable of helping

L. loses no time in reporting everything that happens to her and everything that passes through her head

Some people were sitting higgledy-piggledy in the sunny garden, and it seemed to me that if I had to look at them individually I would be unable to tell them apart

April 18

The hairs of brushed dogs hover over the back gardens in the sunlight

That kind of joyless, brutal laughter is conceivable only here in Germany; it sounds like the heavy wingbeats of a big bird, or like fat moths beating against windowpanes

The old couples sit helpless and forlorn over their beer mugs, looking furtive and sipping the beer that "used to be good"

I look at the people on the shaded terrace, and the only thought that comes to my mind is: Damn riffraff

Easter stroll: the longing to see someone at work in this walking-the-dog-sweater-round-the-waist landscape; or at least someone writing

An old couple are sitting on a bench with a poodle between them, two mounted policemen are talking about me with a smile on their lips, because they see me writing; they make a cyclist dismount, and he continues on his way, pushing his bicycle; they are really on their high horse, and they're not even ashamed, they will never be ashamed, and the walkers walk on the footpaths and they never stand still for a minute, and when the next cyclist comes along, it's the walkers themselves who say "Bicycles forbidden!" and walk and walk with their dogs and their dog licenses

A girl joins a friend at her table and before even sitting down takes a cigarette out of a pack that is lying there

A sadness, as though my fear of death were no longer acute, but still mildly present

Watch a game of ping-pong without turning one's head or even one's eyes

The child already has the same difficulties as a grownup with time and with other people; she runs aimlessly around the garden with the other children, stops, goes through the first motions of a game, but then breaks off in bewilderment; standing still, she does pathetic little imitations of the other children's activity, then makes herself pathetically ridiculous with her attempts at virtuosity, hopping around in a circle, creeping up on someone, spinning on her heel, all this in utter isolation from the others, who have a rhythm of their own; and when once, just once, she is in rhythm with the others and turns to them with a look of pride, they don't notice; even the dogs run away when she tries to bend over and pat them. So she keeps going around in a circle with her hands behind her back, now and then hopping out of her sadness with a pretense at vivacity

The rippling ponds in the closed zoo, the staidly walking, then suddenly running animals, the screams of the peacocks, the big birds running around in circles with wings outspread

Before the onset of twilight, the paths were almost deserted, and now that it's almost dark, people are appearing from all directions

All day long the child has been running around in circles, feeling humiliated, disappointed, sad, and conscious of making herself ridiculous. Now she's asleep and the sighs are still pouring out of her

April 19

I dreamed of my death last night: up until then I had been the hero of my book; after my death I was only the reader

The child, who has fallen down and is bawling hideously: "I can't do anything any more! My luck is gone"

Early morning: already the path outside my window is crunching under the steps of walkers, and the dogs are barking at each other

A.'s habit of calling my attention to every trifle and repeatedly to the same one is an expression of her isolation, also of embarrassment and lack of language

Alone with the glugging of the dishwasher

The sunlit young leaves gleaming out of the shadow—as though hovering in mid-air, with branches

The comforter (the church) has no eyes for those it comforts

Moments of tragic feeling in the purest sunshine: I drop what I am holding

Simply by learning to keep silent, he rid himself of many things that were not his nature but his past

Read *The Promise* by Dürrenmatt: I feel the need to thank him for this project of a life not dominated by the facts

April 20

Noticed: that when I ring Madame L.'s doorbell, she opens immediately, as if she had done nothing but wait for goodness knows how long; that at table she keeps turning the side of the platter that still has something on it in my direction, without saying a word (I must throw off this habit of saying "notice" all the time)

No matter how far away he is standing, no matter how absently he seems to be lolling around, W. hears every word that is said and sees every movement

A small stone, which A. gave me "for luck," falls out of my pocket; I quickly pick it up and put it away. Afterwards I'm proud of having been superstitious

It occurs to me that only what is written by sons or daughters of the petite bourgeoisie or the proletariat (but not proletarian literature) can still arouse my curiosity

"Time the healer"—but what if time itself is the disease?

The human dignity of the past tense: more and more, story-telling strikes me as the only adequate mode of speech

"Only his immediate presence could comfort her, but that comforted her fully, and his presence alone sufficed; no word, no gesture, no touch was needed, only the mere fact of being together. Then they were not two persons but were one person in perfect, unreflecting well-being, content with themselves and the world. Indeed, if one of them had been held fast at the farthermost end of the house, the other would little by little, quite automatically and without deliberate purpose, have moved in that direction. Life, to them, was a riddle, the answer to which they found only with each other"

Horribly tired, yet sleep would only be a subterfuge

As if sleep were already raging inside me, as if it were about to turn me inside out, wrap me up and carry me away

No experience of identity today: only of running after myself

April 21

Shopping: all the food is packaged; nothing looks like itself: eggs, milk, cheese, meat, even apples: all packaged

When I go into a store and the salesman welcomes me with a friendly smile, I know all the same that I may be facing a bosom enemy, and so does he

A fat June bug lay cold and stiff on the sidewalk (so they're not extinct, after all)

Looking at a class photograph, I couldn't help visualizing a cross over certain heads

"I love him, and I think he loves me" (an actress in the "People" section of *Time* magazine)

Child's birthday: I eat the leftovers, not because I want them, just to clean up

After hours of wild screaming and not knowing what to do with themselves, the children have managed to get together in a quiet game, and now they are being separated

Now they've started sending drawings instead of photographs from Cambodia—it's like a courtroom where photographers are not admitted

They keep dinning it into us: "The Third World War"; why this compulsive counting?

As I was buying a sand timer, the saleswoman said: "Oh! For the telephone!"

Suddenly finding oneself beautiful: a moment of immortality

What he had formerly experienced as "excitement," "anxiety," "depression," "boredom," etc., he now began to feel chiefly in his body as "pain"; likewise, he felt "contentment," "happiness," "serenity," and "pleasure" in his body as "breathing deeply" (*Old Man Blues*)

Ventilate the apartment by letting a crowd of children run through it all afternoon

Looking into a cellar apartment: on the television screen an elevator is going up

A.'s compulsion to buy something when we go into a store where something was once bought for her

One of my manias: I can't hold anything in my hand for any length of time without wanting to throw it away (even if it's something I need)

Cool evening: the opening where the stamps come out of the vending machine is still warm from the heat of the day

Businesswoman driving home from work: while waiting at a red light, she reads a file that lies open on the seat beside her

Toward evening, the elderly schoolteacher strode stiffly around the school garden, watering the flowers. I have a feeling that this simple observation holds a secret, but one which I can clear up by thinking back (she has never spoken a word of German to me, though I know from A. that she speaks German) and by thinking ahead (in two months she will leave the school forever and go into some sort of unimaginable retirement)

Ferdinand Hodler's painting of a dying woman: tired, closed eyes, mouth open enough to show the upper and lower teeth, not gaping wide, but looking rather demure, almost prim (in retrospect, I had the feeling that the woman was not so much suffering as making a show of suffering; that this dying woman was at once exaggerating her pain and displaying self-control)

"At a very early stage, when matter was still relatively dense, the universe must have been permeable to cosmic radiation; today, in the form of 'diffuse light,' this extragalactic diffuse gamma radiation fills all cosmic space" (write this way about relations among people)

My throwing-away mania is so intense that I always use too much shaving cream, so as to empty the tube as soon as possible and have something more to throw away

The moment I plunged my feet into the warm water, the dividing lines I had drawn in the course of the day and of many days vanished

Testing a feeling: if it repeats itself word for word, I trust it, then I know it wasn't imaginary

Perfect stillness in the room, only the magnetic needle on the table is still trembling

Hesse on Goethe: "Unvarying beauty"

N. and I often laugh rather playfully on the telephone simply because we are telephoning and there are certain things one can't help saying on the telephone (we laugh like two people who are deceiving each other but know it and are amused)

"I didn't love you today"

April 22

Another "full moon": someone has come along and there he is! (The insolence of that big round moon over the rooftops)

I was extremely active yesterday: I walked, bent down, cleaned the house, washed dishes, stood in line, read, thought, talked, drew, wrote—but even then I was not *honestly* tired

Humiliating dreams: in which it turns out that something one still hopes to do has already been done

In stroking certain areas of her skin I faltered, and stroking became a mechanism or technique (a term from the daily Cold War: "stroking quotient")

Wake someone up by dazzling him with a mirror

I look about for a woman who was running up the steps to the station a moment ago; she has turned into the bird that is just flying up into that tree

Place Dauphine: ". . . *un des pires terrains vagues qui soient à Paris*" (Breton)

My mother used to say: "How the money goes!" I have the same impression, but I'm not desperate about it as she was, only amazed

"I have enjoyed beautiful hours at the theater, but I am gradually growing tired of running this risk of illusion every time I go" (Hesse)

Dislike of going underground (into the Métro) and of flying —apparent need of contact with the surface of the earth

In opening the window, the woman lets out a snatch of the song being played on her record player—but just for this one moment

It would seem as though Hesse could not endure the world as a whole and was in too much of a hurry to convert it into literary forms: ". . . and I made friends with my past" (my own hatred of my past)

Memory and yearning, thought and feeling, body and soul, individual and society seem in poetry to fuse into *one* feeling, an immediate joy of life (but this feeling must be renewed every single day)

Repeated demonstrations of courage have made his chin sag (a racing driver)

Split personality as a solution: the thought that *I* am not doing this damned kitchen work, but someone else, someone famous who is not a prisoner of such work but is doing it in response to a passing whim (e.g., Jack Nicholson or Kennedy!), enables me, for moments at a time, to bear it without difficulty (the origin of schizophrenia)

Packaged meat in the supermarket: the sinews are on the underside

Fantasy: all the innumerable housewives who cut their fingers in the course of the day and lose their adhesive bandages while washing the supper dishes; in innumerable kitchens at this very moment, a wad of wet adhesive bandage is lying beside the dish drainer

To have everything within easy reach (luxury)

"But silence follows
thoughts as
effect follows cause"
(Ernst Meister)

Longing for another color dream

April 23

How often when talking about celebrities people pretend, before naming them, to cast about for their names

In daily life, even when I'm alone, even when there's no other audience, I play myself; and I have no desire to stop doing so; the essential, on the contrary, is to omit nothing from this self-portrayal: every misdeed I have ever perpetrated would be included, reflected perhaps by nothing more than a brief hesitation, but then I would continue in a more enlightened vein or possibly stop "acting" altogether; if I include my own misdeeds in my picture of myself, then nothing in others will be alien to me (misdeeds, inadequacies, will not, as usual, be glossed over, but will form as it were the element of otherness and insight in the daily, vitally necessary game of self-portrayal —the ideal attitude for a writer)

While I am here, I am somewhere else—
ahead or behind
elsewhere another:
Unrest, an unself.
I am only here
I am only now:
I am rest itself

A child who cannot hurry (she makes frantic movements, but takes longer to get things done if one tries to hurry her)

On their way out of the Métro, the people hold the doors for each other; soon they will vanish into their various work holes; the salesgirl in the Métro boutique is slipping on a blue smock over her dress; she, too, has vanished into her hole, although, with her sunglasses perched on her hair, she is still making a show of leisure

In despising your past, aren't you expressing contempt for all those who are still living your past?

The wind on the surface of the water is blowing downstream

A gust of warm air in the midst of the cold blast

A blessing when for a few hours at least there is only the objective world and its presence; cold, warmth, the shadows of clouds, a movie poster; neither anxiety nor euphoria

A break in the film—it hit me like a shot

How quickly my lips dry out when I'm talking to strangers (who keep on being strange)

Hard to summon up feelings for more than one letter a day

"With this wind today," said Frau F., "the children will have to put irons in their pockets" (a phrase from childhood, when irons were still heavy)

Sometimes when I'm affable it's because I'm in a good humor, not because I'm especially affable by nature

The young lady at the bank window gives my dog-eared check a thorough smoothing out

It suddenly occurs to me that if I were just to ask this grumpy woman for something, she would radiate friendliness

And now it's *me* sitting in an airplane, looking down at the hospital where four weeks ago I was watching planes through the window; on the somber earth a box full of wriggling worms

In the strong wind the clouds rose up like fountains behind the rim of the city

What history means to me: something to get rid of

Full of fortitude and self-assurance, I dropped gently off to sleep

April 24

I had just been thinking of this and that; suddenly I caught sight of myself in a mirror and to my surprise recognized myself as the person who had just been thinking of this and that!—whereas some hours before, feeling a certain way and catching sight of myself in the mirror, I had been under the impression that the feeling in my look was put on

Those men in the landscape look like surveyors—maybe the landscape has had it

The sea that we've all heard so much about

During these last few weeks with people I seem to have acquired a new kind of gravity; my convulsions of merriment are behind me

What I like about G.: when her friends are attacked, she doesn't defend them, just shakes her head and smiles; at the most, she says: "No, no"

He sat beside her and said he loved her; she said that excited her so much she couldn't move her hand any more

April 25

A house with sun creams, sun oils, and sun lotions in every bathroom

H.'s favorite saying: "What I like so much about myself is my lack of willpower"

Friedrich Hebbel: "Our celebrated mastery over animals would then amount to this: that we are to them what storms and floods are to us" (my myth of childhood)

"Eyes that glow for no reason at all" (Hebbel on *The Left-Handed Woman*)

I have no desire to learn how to draw—I just want to put certain things down to keep them from slipping away

The warm feeling of not having to talk, of glancing at the sea or doing nothing at all and just letting the general silence pass over me

April 26

Grew heavier overnight, just from sleeping and dreaming

After a humiliating harangue, someone fires one command after another at his humiliator and demands one act of assistance after another; willingly, appeasingly, the humiliator complies (a one-act play)

I suggested something to the child, gave her some advice, and, uncertain about my own suggestion, waited for her reaction—the child rejected it; but when I repeated the suggestion and immediately turned away, she accepted it as a necessity

A. asked me to write something "bad" about her on a piece of paper she had prepared; I did so ("A. is greedy"). She put it in a glass of water and the paper dissolved instantly

My passion for perception, sometimes—I look forward "to seeing you" (epistolary phrase); but only because I know that I'll notice one thing and another in you (just as I am now "looking forward" to the mothers who will be waiting outside the school, though I find most of them repellently ugly—because when I see them I'm sure to notice one thing and another)

Someone who once tried to earn a living as a writer and is now a successful advertising man says of his profession: "It's just a game, you know!"

I looked straight into the eyes of the old woman in the felt slippers and long coat, but was unable to show her that I saw her; and so, though we had always exchanged friendly glances, we stared into each other's eyes for a time and then turned away forever

A story whose hero is a man in a fashionable, well-pressed suit; he keeps this suit until the end of the story, except that the pockets get baggier and baggier

Instantly my stupid nose picks up the smell of a *strange* child's urine in the toilet

"I'll get sick if an idea doesn't come to me soon!"

The sun shone on me and after a while I noticed its effect; it seemed to quiet me: "I let the sun shine on me"

"My dead friend": how can I call a dead man a friend?

April 27

Without meaning to, I kept pointing my ball-point at things; as soon as I noticed what I was doing, I turned it in a direction "where there was nothing"

The pale green of the leaves in the morning (it's a dark windy morning): like deadly nightshade; vision of sprouting potatoes in a cellar

When I said something to the waking child, it made her so tired she went right back to sleep

I decided not to buy a newspaper for the long trip on the Métro—that way I would learn more

I used to be able to read a book *anywhere*

The sight of a woman who is beautiful at first glance seems to give promise of a pure, unblemished, liberating spirit, and as often as not the promise is false: this kind of beauty is heartbreaking. It never ceases to delude us! (And yet how disappointed I feel when I meet a woman and she is not beautiful at first glance—as though the kind of beauty that is evident at first glance were the highest good)

This woman lying there with her eyes closed, waiting, prepared to surrender herself to "pleasure," heedless of anyone but herself. The impulse to say: "Hey, it's not a cock—it's me!"

Progress: the stupid everyday things I have to do with other people no longer infuriate me; now I laugh at myself while doing them

A woman I had asked to join me in a glass of wine: "Are you trying to get me drunk?"

D. told me about falling into the river when she was three; she remembered her feeling of delight at being suddenly swept away

Her fear of death, she told me, dated from the death of her grandfather, when she was three years old. The body was lying in the room below hers. She never saw it—and the terrible thing was not the fact of her grandfather's being dead but the closed door of the room where he was lying. She had a feeling that the corpse was heavy, and she was afraid it would rise up and infect her, and then she would break through the floor and fall on the body. That accounted for her dominant feeling about sex: heaviness and rigidity—the corpse had been a man. A heavy, rigid man moving back and forth inside her, becoming more and more patently corpselike as he approached orgasm, made her think of death (after she told me that, I wanted her to go home, so I could write about her)

April 28

Carried the image of yesterday's blue sky into my sleep with me—and woke up with it unimpaired

"On the street, in the bright morning sunshine, stood an empty car with its windshield wipers working" (that could be the beginning of a story)

N., like myself, has the habit when talking of reaching into his pockets and for the same reason: embarrassment

What desperate cross-currents! Me walking along in perky good humor, behind me a mother who, without even looking around, is bellowing at her child; and another mother is giving her screaming infant a hurt look. And maybe it will soon be all up with me

After I gave her the money, she was very friendly and sat there for quite a while; I was pasting stamps on a letter and stopped to count them; she told me instantly how many were already in place (years ago I would dutifully spend some time with my grandfather after he gave me the money I had asked for)

Dolls in shop windows look more lifelike from year to year

A short-lived "plague of people" in the eternal universe

Crocodile: an animal which, when full grown, has no enemy

A woman went by and my heart stood still

Looking around in the dark movie house: so many glittering eyeglasses!

The old man has fallen asleep and the film hasn't even started yet

Lying in bed, I felt that I was turning *black* with fatigue

April 29

No sooner had I stepped out on the balcony, where I was assailed by a hellish din, than the lady of the house started telling me what a *convenient* location it was

The *forthright* look of a gymnastics teacher

My tiredness and feeling of inadequacy this morning because of hitting A. She was crying, as she often does, because something wasn't exactly the way she wanted it: this time it was the paper kite over her bed; it seemed to her that the wings had been put on the wrong way. As usual, her tears threw me into a rage, but even while I was trying to reverse the wings, the thought flashed through my mind: If I keep calm now, I'll have accomplished something today. For a moment I had the feeling that I'd be able to control myself, but suddenly, when she went on crying because the wings were still not right, I smacked her on the behind, because I couldn't stand the sight of her tears—and yet I had almost succeeded in getting the better of myself. So my morning fatigue turned instantly, without a thought on my part, to violence, and after that all I could do was keep still. I saw the child sitting alone in the kitchen with her breakfast dish, and the line of her neck and cheek burned itself into me like a brand. I sat down facing her and she started talking about something entirely different, just said any old thing *for my sake*, but inside me there was an unthinking, uncontrolled rage against her that refused to go away

Footprints on the dry sidewalk in the morning sun: someone who stepped off the grass that was wet with dew (after my unwarranted treatment of the child, such perception strikes me as hypocritical, an attempt to mollify myself by taking an attitude of perception)

With strangers (who will always be strangers) I have the feeling that whatever I say in answer to the questions they ask me will be a lie (and that I will have to avert my eyes afterwards)

To lie in the sun and think myself away, breathe myself away, until nothing remains of me and everything is absorbed by the wind and the sun—everything except an infinitesimal point of pain. As I lay outstretched in the sun, my hands slipped out of my pockets; when I opened my eyes, there was whiteness before them; when I closed my eyes, I suddenly, in broad daylight, saw the Big Dipper gleaming out of a green darkness. I stopped breathing, I was very still, I merely existed

When they shook hands while talking to each other, the shaking of their hands made their voices quaver

Carrying her baby, made up with whitish vomit, in her arms, the gypsy woman goes from table to table, holding out her hand, as though collecting debts

A woman's brown hair, which for a moment in the glaring sun I thought to be gray: that could be the beginning of her story, of still another story

Great piles of flowers on the florist's stand, including lilac and lily of the valley, and no smell whatever

Let's face it: every child, including A., is ashamed of its parents, and for no other reason than that they are its parents

Frau F.'s feelings of inferiority announce themselves with the sentence: "I feel so melancholy!" and become acute with the sentence: "My system is deranged!" Whereupon she falls silent for the duration of the derangement

A spoiled American poet-professor with a muffler and a turtleneck sweater

Long-lasting sounds of roller skating outside the window and, later on, tired children with roller skates on their feet sitting on the steps outside the house

April 30

Frau F.: "My lips are thin." — Herr F.: "No, your lips are not thin, you just make them thin." — A.: "My lips are thin, too." — Frau F.: "No, your lips are lovely. *My* lips are thin"

A. drew a picture of Frau F.; she began with the pimple on her face

I drank up my tea in a hurry, as though wanting to run after somebody

On leaving the movie house, ask the usher what the film was all about

Much easier to run around with a dish towel for an apron when I think of Cary Grant doing it in a movie

The "ethics committee" of the hospital is deliberating: *should one or shouldn't one* prolong the lives of "soulless vegetables"?

Frau F. thinks people are more likely to talk to themselves in a big city than in the country

". . . I have been hoping that someone from Calw would come and see me and that through him I would be able to love myself to my heart's content, but so far my wish has gone unfulfilled" (Hermann Hesse's grandfather)

"He has so much imagination it has undermined his will" (a teacher, speaking of Hesse)

I *decided* to lie (and did so unscrupulously)

May 1

The fat man was sitting in the café as if he would never be capable of doing anything else

"We must do away with fear." "Why not do away with the world while you're at it?"

The moment I met that vivacious woman, I was conscious of my cracked lips. She stood in front of me, spoke to me about myself, and cut off my view

I was walking down a Métro passageway with a man I didn't know very well. Up ahead of us a woman was lugging a heavy suitcase. Left to himself, either of us would have offered to help her, but in each other's presence we were embarrassed, as though there would have been something affected, something unnatural about it

I longed to recapture the adventurous strangeness between us

The psychoanalyst said: "I have the impression that you have put certain areas of feeling on ice. You have grown hedges around yourself"

What a relief that thus far none of my presentiments has really been fulfilled; but how awful if I weren't to have any more presentiments

"I can bear anything, anything but love" (Hesse at the age of sixteen)

As an adolescent I did not possess the other, poetic world; I only pretended to possess it, because I had an intimation of it; my pretenses, my poetic phrases were an expression of this intimation, a desire for something I had not yet experienced (my double life as an adolescent)

The analyst said that his preoccupation with God had left him, since Easter, with a pain in his left shoulder; that, he said, was obviously the cross; he had been stigmatized

"I'm not 'closed in'—you people close me in with your communication mania!"

When I have no feeling for the person I am talking to, I take more pains in forming words, but I do not succeed in talking louder or more intelligently; I tend to become more inarticulate than usual

May 2

Nearly all my images of childhood have taken on a cool static beauty; in them I myself am a rigid, lifeless something, a mere accessory to the image

Recapture and preserve the circumspectly beautiful life style of the older literature

Some people speak of "thinking" only in connection with their worries: "I've been thinking!"

For most people, "reality" is just another word for trouble

Suddenly I see the light-colored cars crossing the little black bridge over the railroad tracks. I've been living here for more than two years, and I'd never noticed them before. Sometimes I see nothing for months, and then when I do occasionally see something, it becomes a kind of apparition

Happiness—and with it the anxious feeling that it's an exception

In the bus: the passengers as embalmed victims of past catastrophes

"Riding in trains, changing, changing again, riding up and down escalators—in the unceasing, hectic motion of the rush-hour traffic the smell of your hair was all I had to sustain me"

I told the analyst that to define people as "sick," as one of his colleagues did, struck me as arbitrary. He replied that it helped people to hear themselves defined in what was to them an unusual way, since "society" or the state had thus far defined them only as "marginal," "delinquents," etc., and treated them accordingly. That seemed reasonable enough, but what an irony if the only way of giving people a sense of their worth is to define them as "sick"

"I couldn't say who I am, I haven't the remotest notion of myself; I am someone without antecedents, without a history, without a country, and on that I insist!"

May 3

Someone attacked me and I shot him in the face; so then he took on someone else's face, didn't know me any more, and left me alone

Waking up in the morning without a thought in my head and having to begin the day right away—it makes me cranky and unjust

Someone breaks into a jewelry shop to steal the beautiful lavender cushions the jewels are bedded on

While waiting in shops I try to move very cautiously for fear of making the salespeople nervous

Some escaped convicts were hiding in an empty villa. They washed with only a few drops of water for fear of making the slightest sound in the sewers; this was a country where even sewer sounds were monitored

I pretended to be ignorant even of things that everyone knows; this enabled us to make conversation

A film that begins with clouds of dust in the middle of a crowd

Toward evening the sun came out for the first time that day, and everything became very clear, very bright; the small tree in front of the other trees on the edge of the city was a lighter green than anything else, ever so luminous, swaying in the strong evening wind like a helicopter about to take off, something living against the dark green of the mere vegetation

The doorbell rang, but when I opened the door and looked around, there was only the scent of perfume (the beginning of a story)

I was really tired, but also using my tiredness as an excuse

I looked at the clear night sky with the little yellow clouds and the stars, and already I was furious with myself, thinking how quickly I would forget this unique sight

May 4

Strange that people living in a foreign country first learn its blasphemies, obscenities, and fashionable slang, and otherwise remain largely speechless (a girl who has been in Paris only a few months has begun to exclaim in French when she stubs her toe; now she cries *"Aïe!"* instead of "Ouch!")

Neil Diamond: "When I played in small clubs in Greenwich Village, the sound of ice cubes in a glass was as nerve-racking as the scraping of chalk against a blackboard"

Standing inactive in the sun, just turning my head now and then when I heard a sound, I suddenly felt like a bodyguard

The young, still unknown painter had a rigid gaze that perceived nothing but an inner vision or his own disappointment with that inner vision, and when I left him I had a lump of undigested French fries in my chest

"If you start taking that unctuous tone again, I'll cut your throat!"

Defiantly the woman in the café butters her bread, enjoying a brief respite from her routine unhappiness

Walking around my own apartment, I closed off my face as if there were an enemy lurking behind every open door and I didn't want him to see my true face

A young woman whose face when at rest expresses passionate grief

"Can't you stop making those contemptuous digs! All the energy you waste on contemptuous rage—why not save it for a serene love?"

"Little by little I am discovering myself"; that only means: little by little I am finding out what I am *not*

So lively, that policewoman regulating the traffic, putting her white gloved fingers to her lips and blowing kisses at a baby— and yet it wouldn't surprise me in the least to see her stone dead the next minute

The thought that I will probably fail in my frantic daily search for the common denominator of (our) life—but that someone somewhere is bound to succeed: the evening sky; by now the buses circling around the square are almost empty; this is the hour when the cabs line up at the taxi stand, when children are supposed to be asleep but aren't, when truck after truck drives out through the city gates, when the cooks at the restaurants are getting ready to go home, when, lit by street lamps, the round-cropped plane trees look like pagan idols, when people are overcome by a kind of passing fatigue that makes them hard of hearing, and they ask one to speak a little louder

Today, when a whore accosted me, I managed to give her a friendly "No, thank you"

Most of the day I was one among many, but not in the good sense: I looked on with an open mind, but painlessly—without *participating as a witness*

"We share the same past!" — "So what! That's no reason to get familiar"

May 5

Woke up too late, then jumped out of bed, barely able to function. What happened last night? Nothing; at least I don't remember; stupid way to start a day

The water in the gutter appeared to be flowing rapidly; I threw in a piece of paper and walked along beside it; the water was indeed flowing fast, while I strolled easily beside it

Imagine having to look into such big nostrils first thing in the morning!

Just as a child prefers the meals at other people's houses, so I prefer other people's toothpaste

Read some cheerful poems by an American and now I'm all alone with my bad humor

Chestnut blossoms in a puddle of thick black oil

I met a woman who said she had seen me ten years ago, said I'd been very skinny and worn velvet trousers. This woman had been everywhere. Wherever she went, she'd mixed with the natives to learn their way of life; she'd done everything "one does" (and even written "books," by which she means filmscripts). Now she was in Paris "making contacts for a chap I've known for ages." She lives in the country with a "physicist" and a "sociologist"; they have a hen that occasionally lays an egg. Suddenly I felt the need of a drink, whereupon she had an impulse to buy a head of lettuce and an avocado. She talked and talked, about everything she had done, was doing, or was meaning to do. When I asked her if she didn't spend some of her time just "lazing around," she was seriously indignant. I told her it seemed a pity that so many inactive people (some of them inactive by necessity) should feel the need to talk about their thousands and thousands of occupations, and pointed to the shining example of Robert Mitchum, who, when asked what he was doing at the moment, replied: "Nothing. Just lolling around by my swimming pool as usual." I left the woman as soon as possible, saying perhaps we'd meet in another ten years. Her voice had the same calm, extra-soft, lukewarm, unfeeling but feeling-simulating tone as all nondescript hangers-on (of the art world) who were once *political* but have now become *spontaneous* and *sensitive*

While waiting for someone, a woman swung her hips *petulantly*

A. didn't like the food, but it made her so angry she ate it quickly

Watching a group of tourists moving back and forth made me so tired that my eyes closed

Suddenly in the rush-hour Métro crowd I was happy to be squeezed in with other people

When I think I recognize someone on the street: a moment of terror

"A time comes when the most beautiful woman, even a dream woman, has to stand in the street, waiting for her dog to finish shitting"

An ageless face with old teeth

If only a wave of love would surge up in me!

She has had an *experience* and now she is sitting there so solemnly that I'm reluctant to ask her about it

May 6

A stamp lying on a pocket mirror

Experience of the sun, of heat, and of my own strength; I move against the heat as against a strong wind: I'm stronger

Two women were standing side by side; one was looking at a questionnaire with questions to be answered *oui* or *non*. As I passed, I heard her say "cancer"; then I saw the two women take a step away from each other and laugh

The heat had really become a "weight"; I felt that I couldn't think anything "out" any more (as though in the heat nothing remained of language but the clichés)

The park and the chestnut trees: beside every tree a person is sitting motionless, as though part of the tree

The film moved me. Then on the way out I was sidetracked by the soft behind of the woman ahead of me

May 7

When from my half-sleep I fell back into my dream, all the images lost their beautiful earthy heaviness, broke away from me, and took on a life of their own

A stooped old woman with shopping bags was coming toward me. At first glance I thought it was the old schoolteacher (this was her neighborhood). It wasn't, but then I thought: It could have been her; and a moment later: It could be her. It would have been possible to tell her story without really knowing her. The possibility of writing in this way about *others*; the legitimation of fiction

The black trousers of the man ahead of me were covered up to the knee with light-colored spots made by the tongue of the dog running along beside him

Standing in the sun with children by the ice-cream cart: intense memory, not only of the ice cream of my childhood but also of my childhood desire for ice cream: a radiant moment!

"You only come home to go to the toilet!"

Formula for starting a conversation with a woman: "Your life is hard, isn't it?"

I read the headlines about the earthquake in Italy and when a woman beside me clears her throat I hear the sound as a sob

The coins in the window of the newsstand, burning hot from lying in the sun

Writing things down makes one so terribly forgetful

The Métro car in the evening rush hour. The whole strap covered with hands, and my hand at the very top

How to be subversive: accept suffering with patience and contempt (apart from running amok, this is the only attitude I can regard as political)

Strangers in the house: like having scaffoldings all about that hampered my freedom of movement

The parts of my body no longer touch one another:
no toe touches toe
no leg touches leg
no arm touches my head
no finger touches finger
lip no longer touches lip—
only my eyelids touch my eyes
(peace)

May 8

In a dream I said: "She wants to experience something, if only in a fold of her pleated skirt"

All at once, despite the pain, I felt a self-assured *contempt* for death

While bathing in the sea, I saw an airplane coming in for a landing touch the waves, lurch, shoot up into a vertical position, and then sink. I saw the fuselage going under, saw the immobile faces at the windows. Embarrassing! (As a child I had hoped that a plane would crash nearby to make our part of the country interesting.) And this afternoon I'm flying to Los Angeles

A screaming child was pulled away from the window and taken deep inside, until it could no longer be heard

Yesterday D. going home alone: bent, stooped, his hands clasped behind his neck: I *noticed* him

A picture postcard from the Bahamas with the words: "I think you would like it here." Is this intended as an insult?

While packing soft things in my suitcase, it flashed through my mind that in case of a plane crash they would cushion the shock

The cries of the birds looking for their young sound as if the birds were imitating people imitating birds; fear for their young makes animal voices sound human; the wee little answering voice of the chick fallen into a bush sounds like a policeman's whistle filled with water

Kicking the football in the tall grass, which suddenly gives off a strong smell

Read about a couple who worked together; in an American magazine, to boot. Yearning for an ideal world (I want to be fooled)

"At last she came in, radiant with charm"

May 20

From now on, I mean to justify everything I do with the words: "What do you expect? War is war"

A child, wiggling its tongue for pleasure

My first day back in Europe; I've got all the simple little movements right

Some (French?) women in every walk of life seem to have all the routines down pat; for instance, when they close the shutters at night and all you see is their fingertips. Actually, "bourgeois" is just another word for "loathsome"

May 21

The landlady: every day that she doesn't take in money with her apartment she "loses" money (and her young daughter is just as insanely sensible)

A film dark with costumes

"Reality"—a euphemism for anything that prevents one from living

How boring it is to eat cherries when you haven't climbed the tree and picked them yourself!

In my usual environment I notice more than I do in unfamiliar places

Leave the television on, come back hours later and find it perfectly natural that the same thing is still on the screen

The trembling around the woman's lips: her inner monologue

"I can't say anything about him, because I know too much about language" (but he has plenty to say about me, and people believe him)

May 22

Looking at the child, I recall the painful distance I felt as a child between myself and a beloved grownup only a few steps away

I laughed at the sigh that I had just heaved without meaning to

Sing instead of screaming (out of disgust)

A. and I find no difficulty in being friendly to each other now; we have just taken a long, difficult trip together

I insert my ticket in the slot and pass through the turnstile. An electric sign lights up—*"Reprenez votre billet"*—and I think: Some nerve, talking to a total stranger!

Sudden desire to fall into an open manhole. Just for spite

As I walked along, what was dead in me opened up to experience ("I emerged from myself")

Become so unapproachable, so severe, that all other images of me cease to be possible

The headlines that pursue me wherever I go! A little woman trips across the street in front of me, and my rage attaches itself to her, as if she were responsible for such nauseating phrases as "The impending divorce of . . ." "The late-found happiness of . . ."

Shaken up in the Métro, along with others: oh, shelter me; oh, take me in!

Suddenly, in the dark, empty corridor, someone long dead appeared to me as a smile; I returned the smile

Learn to manage without music

Her eyes had been deprived for so long that they instantly absorbed the first tears

A woman who, to prepare herself and others for any (to her) noteworthy activity, removes all the rings from her fingers and puts them on the table

Inexplicable memories, disturbances in the flow of the day; but of course they are part of the day

Everyday version of *The Marquise of O.*: someone unknowingly gets a knowing woman with child

May 23

The stupid things she had said the night before tormented me the following morning as if I myself had said them ("Such a gentle young fellow, so blond!" "To lie in bed with someone when there's nothing between you, oh, how lovely that can be!")

If only I could find it easy to get along with children, for just one day

Slight anxiety when the strange woman at the door turned out to be "not bad-looking"; relief when her stupidity became apparent

D. on the subject of men with tense stomach muscles: "Afraid of giving themselves away"

The child was crying with all her might but at the same time listening to make sure we were all reacting suitably; when I laughed, she stopped crying and bellowed with rage

When little N. speaks, she takes the tone of one who is always being scolded and reprimanded but wants what she wants all the same. When she heard over the phone that her father was ill, she began to scream; her mother asked me to give the child a hug, she loved her father so. When I went over to comfort her, she was blowing soap bubbles with utter concentration (in watching this child, I felt no affection—and this amazed me; it seemed almost inconceivable that one could watch a child without feeling affection)

One of those rare days when I miss my aim in throwing

My distaste for voices that are as "clear as a bell" (Joan Baez)

I was looking forward to the mere sight of her

For children there seems to be no gap between knowledge and existence: in their existence, their games, they draw on what they know; whereas my little bit of knowledge is of no use to me in my daily existence (Goethe, on the other hand, was helped by his knowledge; trickery?)

Taking leave of a little boy, A. tilted her head a little and closed her eyes for a moment in an incredible gesture of silent affection

I said: "Instead of eating lunch here, we could take some food with us and eat in the open." "You mean a picnic?" I: "Don't use that word." She: "Funny—you like the thing but not the word." I: "If you use the word, I won't like the thing any more" (I feel the same way about words like "hike," "meat," etc. . . .)

Spending the whole day with an ugly person: such ugliness seems *malevolent*

Close to tears while reading about a heroic football game

I felt so confident that there was a singing in my head; the leaves began to rustle and it grew slowly warmer in the cool shade of the trees (the rustling of the leaves just barely sent a shudder over the skin of my arms)

Some people seem to be as beautiful as objects; hairline, neck, nose—everything is "right"; and yet human beauty is undoubtedly different: because they are already beautiful, these people can never *become* beautiful; they can only become ugly and that very quickly, they are easily disfigured, their beauty is always in danger of congealing and becoming ridiculous

This poodle was badly synchronized; the bark and the barking motions didn't go together

My daily bungling, at the housework, at shopping, and now at barbering

The pleasure, while leafing through a book, of noticing by the way some of the pages stick together that I am the first reader

When everyone starts singing in the restaurant, the thought: How pleasantly most people are able to lull themselves with this kind of thing, and it's just a matter of luck who gets left out

Sometimes I wonder how much more I know beyond what I am putting down; I would like to know more than what I am saying—and keep it to myself

He takes another drink of wine before the taste of the last swallow has passed: he shouldn't do that

May 24

The need to be practical makes me inattentive

He knew her and looked into her eyes, but was incapable of showing her that he saw her

The moment I enter the department store I seem automatically, under the neon light, to put on an idiotic face

That woman walking so elegantly through the crowd with her child. You'd have thought she was walking her dog. And then I noticed that it actually was a dog

I begged A. not to make such repulsive faces when she was crying (of course she couldn't help it)

In the evening I feel as if I hadn't done anything all day unless I've thought about someone (so I make myself think about someone)

The well-groomed man who, at the sight of my disorderly mop, automatically runs his hands over his hair

I feel "masculine" and adult because I know I'm ready for a fight

She sighed when I touched the place where she loved herself

May 25

Fatigue kept freezing my thoughts and images; for a few seconds I slept with my eyes open, and then another thought or image set itself in motion; fatigue tugged at me from within, I felt it physically, and wherever it manifested itself it became a pain

Odd how amiably I talked to a friend on the phone, when at the same time there was a stranger in the house with whom I was incapable of talking

Every time we meet, even if only a short while has passed, we ask each other how old we have got to be since our last meeting

A middle-aged woman and a young woman were talking side by side; suddenly the young woman took hold of the older woman's hand and raised it to her lips, as though she needed that hand to console her. Then she released it and the older woman raised her own hand to her lips—only then did I realize that they had merely been smelling a perfume which the older woman must have had on the back of her hand (my tendency to idealize)

A mirror in the church; all of a sudden I saw myself as an angry saint

They tried to stir him up and he just grinned

"Tell me a story about myself; maybe it won't be true—but that doesn't matter" ("I need a version of myself")

After saying something stupid, I thought I deserved to have my plane crash the next day

Despair: the need for something to happen. "Something has got to happen"; unable to endure myself in a static world (the least I can do is *drop* something, or fall down)

Sometimes in the presence of her husband Frau F. speaks like a schoolchild reciting a lesson to a teacher, even when she is talking to someone else; she doesn't take on the schoolchild manner right away, but after talking herself into a muddle she glances at her husband and starts reciting lines as though he were "hearing" her lesson

May 26

Someone said: "Nobody dies of hypotheses"—meaning: we need the old convictions (which are worth dying for)

At last—two bus drivers who pass each other without a greeting

Here (in the South of France) for the first time in years I have seen all the ages of life combined in the face of one young girl: experience of beauty

An inspector catches a boy without a ticket and puts him off the bus: is it possible that even he will someday be given a flattering obituary?

Something to hate: religious bookstores (*"La Librairie de l'Eglise"*)

The lips of women who reply at once if I speak to them in the street (but this one did not feel concerned about a whistle from far off; she did not turn around as I expected, and I realized that I had done her an injustice); but if too much time goes by without anyone talking to them, their lips curl with contempt for all these boring men around them

I used to think that certain art objects freed people from the need for hysterical partisanship and that this was their special quality; but it soon turned out that even they have their hysterical partisans

I noticed how, especially in conversation with strangers, I tend to jump from one subject to another, while other people manage to speak of one thing at a time

A television journalist: "We'd like to hear your opinion." — "But I've neither seen the film nor read the book." "Doesn't matter. We only need a few words"

The man was appealing to me; he went on and on, and I could feel the intensity of his sadness, but though I asked him to talk louder, he spoke so softly that I couldn't understand a word

Amazing that even children should be able to lie so idiotically motionless on their bellies in the sun!

The child, who usually sits so quietly, is still quaking from her recent weeping jag

It's either flabby bodies or those hard athletic ones whose owners keep looking down at them—can't we have something else!

Every form of body strikes me as absurd; if one could only dissolve in the undefinable

If in speaking I were cut off from "As if," what dreary, suffocating inarticulateness (and yet in writing I try my best to do without "as ifs"—*except at the present moment*)

Swimming in the sea, the stranger and I manage to smile at each other for no reason at all

A mottled pigeon suddenly appears on the beach, looking like the sole survivor of a shipwreck

In despair, one seems at least to acquire form; that's what is lacking in mere bad humor, which is absence of form

May 28

When in my restless sleep words kept changing as on stop-watch dials or airport call-boards, and things changed just as rapidly, until in the end no word and no thing remained perceptible, and all I could perceive was the incessant transformation of all words and things, I feared the imminence of death, when all possible words merge into a single jumble and all things into a monstrous un-thing (no clarity, as is usually claimed, at the moment of death; rather, the sickening muddle of madness)

My dreams: objects become plainer and less precise: plainer in their imprecision

"You can't come to me with *every* problem"

Alone with himself, he became wide-eyed: in thinking, in feeling, in being

May 29

He dressed: the terrible news would at least find him with his clothes on

She spoke as if she expected me to take what she said with a grain of salt; it was only when she noticed that I was listening eagerly that her voice gradually changed

Saturday afternoon. A warm rain has begun to fall, the pavement is becoming wet and dark, but the sand under the trees is still light and dry. Three people are sitting on a bench under a plane tree, two elderly men and between them a young woman. In anticipation of a heavier rain, they have spread out a towel on the bench, and there they sit eating chocolate cookies out of a bag

Speaking of a woman with whom he has business relations, he said: "Of course I have to be careful, she's in love with me"

He tires so easily because he uses the same huge amount of energy for everything he does. If it's an activity that doesn't call for so much energy, exhaustion sets in immediately (he is always in a sweat)

Inoffensiveness in a writer: an expression of (secret) guilt

In my fear that the worst had come to pass, the bleak certainty that I was no longer capable even of committing suicide; I saw the afternoon clouds, the green cow pasture, and myself in the pasture, turned to stone; already the electric signs were flickering on the darkening horizon, and once again, as when I drove through the village with its smoking chimneys toward the house where my mother's body lay, I had the feeling that my own fate was irrelevant. But that was hardly a consolation

May 30

Someone who often stops and looks around as though in the course of his customary day an entirely different day were escaping him

On board the plane: the sky above the last streaks of cloud and the perfectly motionless lines of the clouds—a tranquillity that has been wafted away forever

Dread: even in broad daylight, unable to breathe deeply; only flat night breathing is possible

My often enormous reluctance to talk, even when all that's needed is the simplest possible communication

What some people call funny is only a letting-go when one ought to remain serious

Some people are perceptive only in company (then they keep calling one another's attention to something)

Someone must help me to think! (Today)

A danger with me: it takes me so long to express trifling dislikes, even to myself; but once I express them, even to myself, they take the place of the whole person, and as far as I am concerned, that is the end of *him* (or her)

It seems to have become impossible to portray loneliness—except perhaps as very small, in the lower left-hand corner of the picture

I thought of my grandfather, who used to spear a snake on a split stick and then plant the stick with the snake on it in the earth: the earth was his element, while nothing (or occasionally everything) is my element

Sudden darkness—as though the world were offended

"Did it cost you an inner struggle to do that?" — "No, I had made up my mind"

It is not yet entirely dark—the sky still has its beautiful unevenness

The TV theme songs from all the houses roundabout—how at the same time can there be death?

The people arrive in front of their houses after their long holiday trip; they stand there scratching their heads after the hard drive; rather empty-looking plastic bags crackle in the mild evening air, the children still have their loud voices, car trunks are open, and car doors are slamming on all sides

May 31

The wineglasses have all been smashed and the lease has run out—now it's really time to move

With someone I didn't want in the apartment, I began to do the housework *around* him

Skyscrapers and playgrounds: about such things it is no longer possible to have thoughts, not even "critical" thoughts

While passing a dimly lit café, I saw my double again for a moment behind the bar; my fear was too tenuous to make me start, my starting too unreal to be noticeable—I just went on

She doesn't babble, she whines. If she babbled, she would sometimes have the charm of self-abandon—as it is, her talk produces the effect of what we catch when we pass people talking to themselves on the street: sometimes it may actually be addressed to us or directed against us, but whether we hear it or not doesn't matter. With her there is never a pleasant silence: if she is not talking, it means she is angry, offended, or just out of sorts; once that passes, the petty soulless whining starts in again, gossiping, finding fault, as toneless as water without pressure (which reminds me that there was actually a bit of pressure in the pipes today, possibly because there are so few people in town over the holidays)

This afternoon out here beside the railroad embankment and its tall shiny grass, with the light shimmering through the roof of the café terrace—I suddenly looked up and at last I became the world again

"Willingness to remain open to the coming or non-coming of God. Even the experience of his non-coming is not nothing; it is the liberation of man from subjection to existing things" (Heidegger)

Sometimes it seems to me that the much-touted knowledge of history provides nothing but false expectations

Perhaps it is a good thing if, in writing, one no longer feels much desire, but only uses the memory of it as energy for one's characters

My now frequent nightmare: that I haven't learned my natural-history lesson

The panicked physiognomy of an ego—and by contrast the self-assured face of the non-ego

Endure the monotony of everyday life (and not, just for instance, long for a Gestapo raincoat)

G.: "Crying saved me from suicide"

"Let's hope you haven't forgotten anything." — "If I've forgotten something, it will be a sign that I want to come again." — "There are no signs"

G. always sits down on something that I have to pull out from under him

The angular shoulder of a sleeping child

He read the letter that was meant to destroy him and said he would soon be going to America for good

In talking, G. often jumps so from one thing to another that it makes me dizzy and my dizziness makes me insensible to G. as a person

June 1

My stilted tone in the morning when I tried to talk A. out of her tiredness—sympathy as a mere technique; it was only after giving my voice a jolt that I began to talk seriously; but even then I kept suddenly changing my tone, because I noticed that I was in danger of lapsing into a routine

The office she works in means nothing to her; but she gets "her phone calls" there

Air. I was going to make words with it, but then I answered by blowing it out through my nose

A grownup asked a little girl the color of her eyes, and she told him. How did she know? By looking in the mirror, she replied. "Coquette!" said the grownup

June 2

Her gait fits her speech: she walks with the front part of her feet and she speaks with the front part of her mouth

The ice cream in the glass case—it didn't have those deep furrows in it this morning (visible passage of time)

Dinner in a French family: though the wine bottles are almost empty, they are recorked and taken away; son and daughter listen with the same downcast eyes—hard to say whether from distaste, fatigue, or concentration—to their father's talk; with his eyelids lowered, the son looked dead

A hush-hush woman: hush-hush as a form of existence (have a whispered confidence ready for every eventuality); she probably falls asleep at night muttering confidences introduced with such standard formulas as "Have you heard that . . ." "Did you know that . . ."

We had so much to say to each other so quickly that when we finished we could only sit there making swallowing sounds

June 3

I have had to wait too long for my feeling to take on body; now it has become an idea without feeling

"My girl friend is so beautiful there are times when I can only stand and gape"

I often derive my sense of freedom from someone else's lack of freedom

I opened the newspaper, and my mind started to wander

The man beside me is writing, too. Suddenly he looks up suspiciously; is he afraid I'll copy his business notes?

June 4

The meadow in the evening sun: all nibbled bare by words, nothing perceptible (only a single "white spot")

Finally, in the afternoon, he remembered who he was; for that one moment he managed to feel identical with himself, and then, at last, he no longer thought as poorly of himself as he had for a long while

Why do people persist in searching their past history for an explanation or even a justification of all their sensibilities, needs, and yearnings—as if they needed explanation or justification?

Once again I entered the house where I had been so often in the course of the years, with the old, rather musty smell of lavender (bathhouse smell), and instantly the thought became intense that I would someday enter into the same smell and that the house would in the meantime have become a house of the dead

The voice of a child in a house ordinarily inhabited only by adults

June 5

Shooting at people all night; woke up with my skin peeling

Admittedly I sometimes hopped and skipped as a child; so my childhood can't have been all that bad

"I'm not tired. I'm not tired." — "I'm tired myself"

June 6

Standing in my shoes, without self-assurance. Makes my feet cold

Alone and not alone: in my own aura

Time and again the need, as a writer, to devise, to invent myths unrelated to the old Western myths; I seem to need new, innocent myths culled from everyday life; myths that will help me to begin *myself* all over again (no more Alexandrian playing with myth, as in Joyce and Beckett)

He spoke so mournfully, and I listened without sympathy: who was to blame?

After the long day together all of us, at almost the same time, suddenly had the feeling that we were not with the right people (but in my case, once I was aware of it, the feeling passed)

A wheel is turning under the silent surface of the earth, and in my half-sleep this glittering wheel suddenly breaks through the earth's crust

June 7

"I can never be alone—someone—my hand, the bridge of my nose, my sweat, my cold feet—is always bothering me . . ."

Meet with friends and take an example from their patience

I: a man without a history, from a family without a history (nothing to take pride in, which is all to the good)

I was so tired that I couldn't make out whether the voice on the radio was speaking or singing

June 8

Better no thoughts at all than thoughts (as so often) just declaiming in my head

The dismal pianos in apartments, like "blind alley" signs

A wish: to look out the window and suddenly see "the linkup" —as in a detective story

Pleasant sensation when my feeling has deceived me

June 9

I saw her, she was very beautiful, and the eyes of my yearning looked elsewhere

In the dusk she gradually became beautiful; that is, impersonal

Took the children to a movie about dinosaurs. Walking home afterwards, A. heard a sound from an open window and thought it was dinosaurs talking; actually, it was wet concrete being shoveled out of a wooden trough (but the sound was right)

Progress: managing to listen to several people at once without apparent effort (and naturally answer the children's questions)

June 10

Looking at Egyptian sarcophagi took away some of my fear of death: comforting to be an ornament inside other ornaments; besides, these sarcophagi are so big one could lose oneself inside

Let's not escape into thoughts about Tutankhamen's golden chariot, about the hammering of gold, for instance, or the time that has elapsed since it was hammered—the difficult thing is just to look

I laugh too much

With me, all duties demand an exertion, a decision—I can't just do them like other people

She said that women, too, should forget their past and stop letting its rules dictate their way of walking in the street

Perfect self-confidence: I can shift the focus of my eyes instantly to any new object, however surprising

A woman screws up her face at the sight of me; if I were to ask her why she can't bear to look at me, she would immediately beam with trustfulness

In the apartment next door the TV is turned so low that the voices suddenly sound real, physically present

The night grew cool, but with the fragrance of the lilacs a last breath of the day's heat wafted in

I feel certain that the general mood in this house is one of peevishness, though I know nothing of the people except the sounds they make, especially in opening and closing their shutters

June 11

Resting my hand on the sleeping child's head, I lost the feeling of corruption, of forlornness, of superfluousness, of expendability that so often sets in at the moment of waking

Days shot through with unclear dream memories, which briefly efface the visible world (both the memories and the outside world lack concreteness)

Difference between clichés in writing and in filmmaking: in writing, they just crop up; in filmmaking, they are created by design and an effort is needed; they are worthy of respect because they require work

My embarrassment in the presence of someone who really believes in God and is permeated by his belief

When the pain set in, I took it as a matter of course; I was surprised that it hadn't set in much sooner

The heat outside and the saleswoman in the department store basement; her cool hand as she put the change into my warm hand

Heavy head in the muggy night

Night. I'm sitting in the garden as still as a raven—suddenly the plants around me in the darkness seem so friendly, so alive, so "faithful"; the lampshades in the colorless room look like the heads of vultures

June 12

My satisfaction at being left alone for a while in a room in someone else's apartment

Harmony of sleep: "singing child"; disillusioned waking: the child is screaming

Pleased with my imperfection

What people say about me: I tolerate it, but it doesn't concern me

He's lucky; anyone can see how lonely he is

The great actor makes either no gesture at all or a big, all-encompassing one; either no glance at all or a long one . . .

Embarrassment, inauthenticity: my horizon is broken

Now he has told me his whole story—what will he do with himself for the rest of the day? (Thought while half asleep)

June 13

The sun isn't up yet and the bees are already in the blossoms, which, shaken by the movement of the bees, fall to the ground; sometimes whole swarms of them, then for a long while none

"In happy souls there is no wit" (Novalis)

Melody in speaking: a way of simulating life; anticipate the possession of something one will acquire only with time

"Every beautiful thing is a self-illumined, perfect individual" (Novalis) — That is why beautiful things seem so calm

For a time, purposely forget something that has caught my attention

Herr F. says: "the fence man," "the roof man," "the stove man," meaning the makers of fences, roofs, and stoves

Sunday night: when the telephone rings anywhere in the building, it is answered immediately

Sunday-evening sounds: the clatter of knives and forks at irregular, leisurely intervals; the creaking of the floor under the slow steps of people getting ready for bed; plates being quietly piled up; the repeated cry of a child: *"Bonsoir, maman!"* (This child wants to be heard, wants an answer just this once)—and then, suddenly, when I thought everyone was falling asleep, a voice, calm but very much awake; a toilet flushing, the click of a light switch; a door which for once (blessed be tiredness) is closed considerately (a tired person's consideration for himself) rather than brutally as in the daytime and all week (a bat just dove past); now only women's voices; the sound of me pouring wine; curtains being drawn with a single movement—a few scattered sounds, very brief, at long intervals, such as objects falling on the floor; my feet shifting their position on the gravel; someone saying: *"À demain!"* Dogs barking in the distance (now at last far-away sounds have become audible); I, the private detective, with no need to notice anything in particular, but authorized to notice everything, the starting of the last cars, the tenants talking as if already asleep. And now at last the whole house is really asleep . . .

C. is going mad because of her failure to get rich

. . . and at last I hear a few leaves moving softly in the bushes; then the voices of people who had been still for a long while and suddenly, without preparation, start up; the sound of tearing Scotch tape; dotlike sounds in the vines on the garden wall—and then suddenly all the waking, workaday sounds resume, as though the previous harmony of sounds had been a sheer invention of mine—but this beginning of day in the middle of the night was a delusion, for now it is quite still again, and even the throat-clearing sound a moment ago was probably made by someone reading in bed; now all sounds, including those on the street, are household sounds (along with the tinkling of the wineglass that is trembling on the metal tabletop beside me as I write): how quickly the cars are starting now! And now I hear a soft crackling in the wall vines, like beetles in the flowers, or like the flowers themselves; a page of a book is turned a floor above me; a cat screeches; the-sound of the coins shifting in my trouser pocket; the soft snoring of the child in the open room; the almost inaudible rustling of the falling blossoms in the bushes, one of which grazes my temple; the opening of a window, as abrupt as if the window had been struck by a stone; a blossom falls on my foot, and the sensation is as gentle and friendly as if it came from my skin itself—"it is not my aim to be one with the world, to lose myself, to melt into the world: my aim is to have no aim!" A blossom grazed my ear, it was like having an earring on it; for a moment cooler air, like a new color; a feverish stillness, rising from nests of flame, which can always flare up anew; blossoms fall in the still night with a sound such as stuck eyelids sometimes make in opening—and only after swarms of blossoms have fallen do I feel the breeze that has brought them down, but then nothing more falls; and the hair on my forehead tickles like spiderwebs

June 14

Thoughts that scalp one gently

June 15

"Kept young by looking in the mirror"

Saw my back in a dream

At the sight of the hair that had been cut off her head, A. cried as if she had lost a beloved pet

Photograph of people standing around a murdered man: not one is looking at the dead man on the ground; all are looking elsewhere or into the camera (the bodyguard, who was also murdered, is holding the thumb of one hand in the clenched fist of the other)

Children all talking at once, using entirely different words to tell about something they have gone through together. When they come to the end of the story, they finish up in unison, all with the same words

A. pitches her voice entirely differently when she speaks French: "I'd speak very badly if I didn't"

My fears of so overwhelming people with my present talkativeness, of sounding so convincing that they will idealize me for a while and then out of aversion for all ideals turn against me and against all talk. An upsetting notion: holding forth, I get people to think that I own the truth. It's always happening to me; in fact, it happened only this evening when, shamed by my persuasiveness, I broke off and pointed at the children outside, sitting so importantly on a bench in the twilight, holding up enormous newspapers in the light of the street lamps

The *patronne* of the restaurant, trying to discipline the noisy children, instead of leaving it to us. I could have killed her; no, not killed, just eliminated her (so few children have ever set foot in this "picturesque" restaurant that the women who run it can't even tell the boys from the girls)

The sound of clicking nail clippers coming out of the house at night—yesterday the woman who lives there was talking melodiously with her lady friends about the looks of politicians: today she is alone, rhythmically cutting her nails

When I hear a sigh from one of the windows of this building, I always interpret it as a sigh of unhappiness, not of relief, let alone of well-being (inconceivable)

Suddenly my trouser leg uncoiled like an animal—like a snake, I thought, but without feeling it (that's why I wasn't frightened)

A child crying frantically coughs and calms down

Windows are pushed open so violently in the hot night that they tremble for a long time afterwards

June 16

At first the young painter wandered aimlessly about with his full knapsack. Then finally he decided to go in the direction his knapsack took him: he needed these symbolic hints for all his simplest actions. On his way to India he had bashed his forehead, and he was convinced that the scar had the shape of some object which he had chosen as his symbol while in India. Wherever he went, he rediscovered his symbols. How boring he seemed with his obsessive need to translate the world into his own terms; when with him, I wanted nothing but plain, unsymbolic everyday life. And the worst of it was that he wasn't mad, he just had a weakness for hackneyed symbols

I greeted the woman in passing, but she was gone before I squeezed out the smile that should have gone with the greeting

Her crying is just a louder breathing

Now in the twilight garden I immerse myself in my momentary feeling to save it from the threat of meaninglessness, to give it a meaning that will need no one else, no other judge but me alone, while above me a woman clears her throat, and my pondering sends a pleasant warmth into my feet

Thought: When most people speak or write they degrade themselves and others (speaking and writing as betrayal in a two-fold sense)

June 17

The appetite for the whole world that sometimes comes over me when reading about other continents, as just now, for example, in reading the words: "California weirdness"

The very word "reality" is a euphemism; to use it, even in a critical sense (the "demands of reality"), would be to give this obscure "reality" a prestige it doesn't deserve

Dangerous sense of well-being, in which I can conceive of other people's unhappiness but not enter into it; exasperated by this sense of well-being on this airy sunny day

A day when work sounds are ingredients in the general atmosphere of peace

I realized that though I enjoyed my friend's company I was glad to be rid of him, because I wanted to think about the day and to formulate my observations

Night in the garden: I tried to make my friend moderate his voice by speaking softly myself, but was relieved that he failed to take my hint

G. doesn't even know when he feels uncomfortable; he is aware of his discomfort but doesn't *feel* it (just goes into various contortions and scratches his head and shin at the same time)

Give her my body to taste

Since I am nothing definite, I can think beyond myself

June 18

A night so charged with dreams, whirring, booming, so shot through with movement, and in the end devoured, absorbed, that I didn't for one moment have the usual feeling of sleep

A conversation about a movie (*Taxi Driver*) has sufficed to make two "good friends" aware of what they suspected at the very start of their acquaintance, without wanting to admit it; namely, that they have nothing in common and will always be strangers, if not enemies

I showed the friends who owed me money my new suit. I thought it would ease their conscience

A beautiful girl with bare shoulders entered the Métro car; at first the other women seemed vexed—but then, as they looked at the girl and took a liking to her, they seemed to grow younger

The summer newspaper—the sun shines through, as though nothing serious, nothing menacing could happen at this time of year

I must gear my thoughts to the few moments each day when the painfully speechless, stammering world speaks clearly

He can't bear the sight of sunburnt people, because his mother, who died of cancer of the liver, had that brownish color before she died

Branches at night, moving up and down as unnaturally as cows chewing their cud

As I scrutinize this past day, the greater part of it has the appearance of an empty honeycomb

Explicit stupidity may, after all, be a proof of existence: with its undissembled inadequacy, it shows a need to manifest itself, to be present, to join in the game; stupidity as expression of an affliction that does not yet know itself—perhaps if one were to shoo it gently away from the affected person, one would discover a long sorrow

June 19

I can't summon up any half-sleep images today; it's as if I had failed an examination

As though the garden were on fire with birdcalls

1 4 4

"Something or other was somehow moving in front of my whatsit." This is exactly how I sometimes feel about the world

False half-sleep images, which I *produce* instead of letting them happen

In my half-sleep I and my cramped limbs become a rack in a tiled operating room

On the way to the seashore: the landscape is really "under the sky," bedded in the firmament; one can equally well say "underneath" or "beyond" (feeling of the unity of heaven and earth)

My old familiar boredom in the hotel room by the sea. It will be dissipated in walking, looking at things, etc. But one day, perhaps, this boredom will settle in for good and never go away

For the last few hours two boys and two girls (fourteen or fifteen years old) have been playing in a small area on the beach. All their actions (hugging, hitting one another, hanging on one another's neck) are merely hinted-at, quick movements without continuity. The same is true of their talk, their cries, their glances. They seem to be spending the whole day in such little symbolic rituals, a strange composite of karate films, porno films, adventure films. A pirate carries a woman in his arms; a woman sets her foot on a man's neck; one man stands on another man's belly; a man playing dead is awakened by a slap in the face. Most of the time the girls look on (simultaneously playing the role of onlookers) or only enter into the action with their fingertips, or recoil with a play of pent-up lust when the boys bellow at them, or playfully caress the boys' bodies for the merest moment. When this quick action (as quickly changing as that of a troupe of acrobats) threatens to take on the tenderness of normal children, one of the boys makes a hideous face, lets out a karate yell (more like a snarl), and transforms the "threat of tenderness" into a mime of violence or enslavement (or he himself plays the slave with gestures of extreme abjection). Amid these changing tableaux a strange (and strangely beautiful) stillness sets in when one of the boys has to rub the sand out of his eyes, but then he falls to his knees again, throws his head back, and roars with bared teeth; or takes a girl by the neck and shakes her; or grabs her by the arm and drags her through the sand; or the women "come running to separate the fighting men," and in the end one of the boys lets a girl remove a "thorn" from his foot

Alone on the beach in the evening sun, the woman stripped her clothes off and ran into the water, dipping first one shoulder, then the other; I felt a longing as I watched her, and because this woman could not be my longing, my longing turned to pain

My heart palpitates when I think and feel faster than my proper rhythm. Perhaps my rhythm is that of the tides, of the clouds in the sky, of the slowly falling dusk, of the approaching waves, of the wind blowing a shimmer of water across the sand; and perhaps I can attain it by breathing, by looking at my shoes, by waiting, by breathing less and less, and by projecting myself into these activities

Herr F. bought a warm waffle for his wife and carefully carried it, coated with powdered sugar and jam, to their hotel; glancing at the waffle, he said (referring to his wife): "She's such a dear!"

A. was blissfully happy, alone in the enormous hotel room, reading in the twilight, listening to the music and the sound of the sea, with a glass of something to drink on the bedside table—I could *feel* her bliss

When it's low tide at night, the sea seems congealed; and the sound, too, is as monotonous as a broken phonograph record. (From time to time I stop breathing and wait, for fear of dissolving in the people I'm with and losing consciousness.) The evening star seems to hover below the night clouds. I feel so good I want to walk backward. Little exhaust clouds in the sky: what a joy being able to look at them for hours without speech-drained hopelessness, barely breathing the night breeze, which blows as steadily as on the deck of a ship. What a pleasure, waiting for the moment when I shall be able to say: Now it is really night all around me! (The sky is still reflected in the rain puddles.) There's still a bit of color in the clouds, the color of an overboiled fish. The light spots grow smaller and at the same time change in shape. Midnight: the spots pale and at the same time glitter in the almost uniform night sky. After midnight: now the brightness is in the waves

June 20

In my childhood I felt deprived because Austria was not on the seacoast (and tonight this mighty roaring in the room)

Even to people only a few feet away Frau F. waves and makes signs

Once again, after hours of being shut up in myself, the world appears to me for a brief moment as a liberation (in the form of houses, clouds, swaths of sand on the beach); and then the gate closes again

Herr F. says (because elections are being held in Spain): "This is a historic day!" Historic days make me sick

Because no luxury is complete, every luxury leaves me with bitter disappointment

The green of a field, so intense that it instantly became "my" green: my eyes were needed to make the green countryside green

Herr and Frau F. with their professional readiness for communication (or call it meddling)

I am accessible to criticism only within the limits of my ideas of myself

"Try scratching yourself in a different direction!"

Moved out of the apartment, leaving no trace behind, feeling that I had escaped once again (and when I switched off the last light, I was not struck down by the always dreaded electric shock)

My power to identify with myself, with my gestalt, with my life, is always failing me—and I make no attempt to overcome this periodic failure of self-identification: I need these calamities

Today I've been moving as in a half-sleep, an unpleasant, fearful half-sleep. The world seems neatly ordered and much too close to me (and yet for the first time in many years I have just eaten an ice-cream cone as I walked in the street)

In a traffic jam on the way back from the seashore: rage thrashing around inside me like a ferocious little animal

My friend's widow is unemployed and always extremely punctual. She comes in, sweats, sobs, talks, leaves—and I, once again undecided about my feelings, arrange my face in various expressions of false sympathy before finding the right one . . . The dignity of her despair, the way she said that alone she had no feeling of herself, no longer knew who she was

It would be best to see no faces for a while; then I wouldn't have to start thinking about them

The people in the bus: cradled around the curve; thoughts of death

If I control myself just once in the course of the day, I acquire patience for the difficulties to come, and this patience, for a certain time at least, requires no self-control

A Moroccan stopped me on the street and spoke of my books. He said that I treated language like a subject people—and that pleased me (royally)

Sex: the ultimate enmity

The dying woman's husband was walking in the street with his little boy; he held the child by the hand, but not in the usual way; he held the child's hand up as they walked, raising it to his own level

To be alone; to be with children; to be with grownups; with me, unfortunately, one of these situations does not easily merge with the next (whereas for some women it is all so natural)

In the playground: some girls are jumping rope and a little boy stands spellbound, watching them. His mother shouts at him, telling him to go somewhere else, she can't bear to see him with a group of girls

The park policeman holds out his bunch of keys like a tommy gun

The woman with cancer: her mouth distorted with pain

The children who have found a path through the thicket: *"C'est notre nouveau monde!"*

While I lose myself in the moving grass, the grass, on the contrary, seems to come into being and to grow with me

June 23

When A. is angry at someone, she wants to steal something from him

One of the mothers at A.'s school scolds her child for spilling something in the car, and then, slumped over the steering wheel, starts sobbing aloud

Fantasy: maybe at the end of the school year the dying woman's husband will ask me for my address, wanting to send me the death notice during the summer vacation

A great actor: one capable of having a feeling quietly, all by himself, and later having it again, for others

On the last day of school A. wept bitter tears. "Where does it hurt?" — "All over"

"If we make an exception for you, we shall have to make an exception for the next person, etc." — "If in this case you take nothing into consideration but the rule, you will have to look for a rule in the next case as well—in the end you will be a slave to rules, and that will be the death of you"

June 24

"I didn't invent this rule, I don't even like it. But if we make an exception for you, we shall have to make one for the next person, too."—"That would be splendid—then this rule you didn't invent and don't like would cease to exist"

She said: "You are so deeply immersed in life, that's why I can tell you everything" (that, too, made me proud)

Fantasy: the disagreeable clerk becomes suddenly friendly when he sees that I have the same ball-point he does (as though we came from the same village or had both served in the field artillery)

I go on talking while passing through the revolving door of a luxury hotel. That'll show them

In my rage at the quietly cold women at the airport counters, with their voices that are not calm but merely dead, I wanted to kill them; no, not kill them, just see them transformed on the spot into something horrible, into the brutal monsters they actually are (I was pleased with the coldness of my rage)

When G., who had been moved out into the corridor with his bed as punishment, masturbated for the first time, he felt a "godlike clarity": his experience of self

"You're so realistic." — "That comes of driving a car"

Cheerfully prepared for every sort of fiasco, I left my hotel room freshly coiffed and wearing a white suit (despite the white suit, no desire to hide how sad and tired I feel)

Arrived at nightfall with sticky clothes and sticky eyelids in a hot, stony, sticky Italian town

No one's indifference to others can be justified by such arguments as: he's only an underling and his superiors treat him just as badly as he treats the public: responsibility should be absolute, no nonsense about the whys and wherefores

In the middle of the night a window is closed in a high-rise building at the other end of the square. Vision of Nosferatu or Batman wrapping himself in his cloak

June 25

No, I will not swear off fantasies; I'll smile at them the moment they appear

A shirt that seemed very dirty when I was tired late last night looked clean enough to me this morning

The cars down on the piazza move slowly, steadily, noisily, as though rolling into battle

Someone who can repeat for the benefit of others a feeling which, if only for a moment, he has had quietly and privately (see above) would be not only a good actor but also an ideal human being

In spending the morning folding shirts, rolling up socks, cutting my nails, bathing and showering, sipping tea from time to time on the balcony, I succeeded for the first time in conceiving of such activity as a possible way of life (for a while)

This cook with his enormous mustache has the concentrated, severe, passionlessly passionate face of a man who takes his work seriously (so rare in younger faces)

A. suddenly took on a look of faraway concentration. To her, thinking means to think of nothing for a while

"Can you laugh with your eyes?"

June 26

Memory: life's most intense experience, after all (looking at walnuts in a restaurant, the duplication which frees me from the present—the memory of a particular path, a particular tree)

My feeling of immortality: my immortality is not in the future, I *have been* immortal now and then

June 27

Sitting in the Piazza San Marco: the feeling that all these people passing by are friends, acquaintances, neighbors from various periods of my life

June 28

How is it possible to achieve such monumentality of expression as the great writers? By living, at times, in reckless disorder

June 29

"Come to bed with me. Right now. It may be boring, but at least it will be unforgettable"

June 30

Now that I'm alone again, I've begun to count everything I do, even my breaths

A. said to me: "You speak Italian the way I swim"

All these filthy people! Alone at last with the air-conditioning

July 1

A woman caught her hand in the door of the railroad car. The way she screamed, I mistook her for a child

A peasant out in the fields is speaking in the kind of voice people reserve for animals

How often in the day, the feeling of definitive failure—and only because all those present have fallen silent, as though each one wished to be somewhere else

July 2

As if one ought to dig into these old churches and tear them apart—not to get their secret out of them, but to give them back a secret

When I caught sight of the man, I was incapable of the slightest friendly look. I took refuge in observation: I observed him

How forlornly, how morosely the curtain flutters in the long tunnel (it's me)

In the course of centuries "without history," Apulia is said to have "succumbed to cheerless monotony" (the people who say such things probably find fault with the words of hit songs)

Another train passed, sending a blast of heat through the open window of my compartment

Separation from a person one loves: every little thing one does becomes a kind of pagan rite devoted to his well-being: even the most trivial action, such as stepping on the flush pedal in the train toilet, takes on a quality of prayer

A day on which apparitions have been mere things, things mere names, and names uncertain—everything has been unsatisfactory, even the sunset

1 5 3

When I look at a picture, I always ask too soon where the crux lies, the question of life and death (my difficulty with painting)

When I go mad, I shall exist uninhabited by myself, without words, without motion

Unfamiliar hotel room, toilet flushing next door: "Even for this sign of being alive, you people are too stupid!"

I switched off the lamp to devote myself to sexual fantasies; tenderness embraced me in the darkness and I dropped right off to sleep

September 1

What a beautiful sentence: "I have forgotten!"

On all sides vulnerable women, obliged to move

A day alone, without activity—and again this overpowering feeling of insignificance: someday I shall just sit here, making faces at empty space. "His unhappiness because he could not get along with people brought him closer to objects (to the tabletop at the café): looking at the tabletop, he gradually regained his sense of self"

September 2

House hunting: I've stopped living; first thing in the morning, smoke on the horizon, maddening heat that makes me rush in all directions and then disappear, but where to?—a woman who has been buried for years in a newsstand, where she can no longer find anything: a sacrifice, I thought; she sacrifices herself for nothing, but still she sacrifices herself

When I see and hear the banality of the lives the people around here have been living—at least to judge by my first impression of the way they talk and act, I understand for a moment how someone can go into politics—in the hope of saving at least his own person from the speechless monotony of private existence

When I followed the clerk out of the agency to look at yet another house, I felt as if a whore were leading me to a hotel

Another suicide apartment for rent: everywhere built-in closets full of clothes (they all seem to take special pride in built-in closets and open them first thing)

Spent the whole day with vultures (agents, landlords, etc.): now at last at the movies, I feel competent again

Every time I said anything F. gave his girl friend a sidelong glance, as though he had told her beforehand what I would be like; each of his glances meant that I had lived up to one of his predictions

The landlord who spends the whole day hanging around the doorways of his various houses

Obstacle to human dignity: a quick temper

F. imitated my way of laughing: a malicious laugh, which I hated in my father

September 3

A phase in which all people would be stricken with elemental disgust and do nothing but roll from side to side, shake their heads, close their eyes, gnash their teeth, and curtain their faces with their hair

Names are ridiculous; why couldn't I have a number instead?

The balloon vanishing over the treetops: so this is death, I thought for a moment

The warm top of a baby's head

The woman who wanted to stay with me spoke insidiously of my "woebegone" face; her hand rested on my back, pleasantly warm; I wanted her to go away

September 4

In his well-cut suit, which he never forgot for a moment, he bent cautiously over the recumbent child, just as in older literature mothers in evening dresses bend over their children, who have already been put to bed

New feeling of remoteness, unconnectedness, of *congealed* beside-myselfness

The dead child's mother sat in the living room, sobbing, and I went out into the corridor with my squeaky shoes

The sky over the flat, faraway horizon, with its clouds lined up in rows like a great, intricate machine

At last I was able again to take a hand in physical labor, without preparations or fuss, and when I finished I no longer stretched out my parched hands as I had done during my interim as a city dweller

A piece of country that has been made hideous and lost its character because everything in it has been given a name and the names have been posted all over

A feeling of well-being set in, as though the world, that inert rectangular plane, had been tilted and upended, and could at last be looked at

September 5

Resolved to spend a day without touching, clutching, short-circuiting myself

I am sometimes active, but active life does not come natural to me; I can manage it only now and then

The idiotic, congested face of a child who has just been refused love

These last few days I've been moving about like a ghost, as though dead—a peaceful feeling

Core an apple with a knife, and out comes the Devil, grinning on the end of the knife

Working in perfect silence: and yet my activity has communicated itself in the form of warmth to the restless child in the next room

The evening horizon, far in the distance, behind the otherwise overcast sky, clouds with glittering edges—a second, miniature · sky

September 6

Once again history has taken on life for me—but once again in a dream of war

A walking dream, in which all life appeared to me; my walk became a journey, my journey an exploration of the world (beautiful madness: to stray so deep into dreams that there's no turning back)

My existence flitted through my tired brain like bats in the dusk: tragic and pitiful

September 7

A married couple who always say "we," even when expressing opinions: "We didn't care for that." The peculiar heartlessness of that "we"

September 8

"The weather changes, the light changes, and so do the movements of things—how can people be unchanging in their hopelessness?"

Inconceivable that one should see a yearning woman "in public" (and just then I saw one)

The door in front of me opens automatically. How amiable!

The woman at the real-estate agency, an absolutely ruthless number, but all charm when her victim hands her a ball-point (or something)

My longing for a desert country, nakedly inhuman, not picturesquely inhuman like France

Repulsive nature: the trees look like cabbages

Photograph of an industrialist's two sons walking behind the coffin of their parents. What if they had no right to their grief? (The embittered faces of the front rows of mourners, the curious faces of those in the rear; the bewildered look of a man off to one side)

September 9

A monkey wrench fell from the scaffolding and hit the sidewalk with a clank: the doorbell rang; I woke up

It's in people that one really sees nature (in A.'s hair, for instance, I see the edge of a deciduous forest)

The sky on the horizon glowing like a blast furnace; an involuntary cry

While walking (or rather plodding) along, D. sometimes gets the idea that a hand will settle on her head and stroke her whenever she needs to be stroked

September 10

On the street. A woman takes leave of a handsome young man, who hurries away without looking back. She crosses the street alone, in a different direction: the desolate, humiliated line of her cheek

Once a day I need nature

Bleakest moment: when a grammatical problem comes up in conversation

An especially dangerous property owner: one who jokes about his ignorance of the laws (this landlord)

"At last I have an ideal: the suburbs!"

September 11

The rain-charged sky is moving rapidly as a whole, all in the same direction; unceasing movement outside the window, although the sky is uniformly gray

So often the cold sensation of looking into another world, in which I was nevertheless imprisoned—but now, with my head propped on my hand, a comforting awareness of seeing my own world in the slanting, fast-falling rain

"A nation that has no history can have no future. Here there is a need for identification" (I identify with the drifting history-less clouds)

A single day all alone with a child is enough to make me feel like a clumsy lummox, as seen by the child; and here I am pacing the floor like a lost scientist

More and more, when I'm alone in a room, I lose the comforting feeling of synchronicity with many other lives and events; more and more, I feel excerpted, totally on my own

Buffeted by the wind, the begonias on the balcony move in jerks like figures in a puppet show

Which is worse: anxiety or people?

On this side of the swaying poplars, bright night clouds racing over the rooftops, halting, piling up, then storming onward: atmosphere of war

The technique of holding a child by the hand

September 12

In the taxi, squeezed against a man with cancer; the feeling that it's contagious

Fell asleep last night without news of the world: the thought that as I lay there unsuspecting, everyone around me had fled and the final catastrophe was at hand—so inaudible had the outside world become, except for the whistling of the wind and the passing of an equally unsuspecting or untroubled figure in a leather jacket

"After a long period of unconsciousness, he found himself again on a sunny autumn morning with a white sky on the horizon and branches opening and closing in front of it"

Two children are talking while watching a Jean Gabin film on TV: "He wants to be dead." — "Now he's all alone." — "Now he has nothing left." — "He'll never say another word to her"

September 13

Managed to ignore the mechanical indifference and contempt of the clerk at the ticket window; immediately after taking my money he slammed his window without so much as looking at me, but I kept cool

Example of a slave to political systems: "When I wrote *La Nausée*, I was an anarchist without knowing it" (Sartre)

In the bus: the young woman's self-control gave her a monkey face

The face of the man at the café table was so sullen he might have been one of the waiters

Catastrophe in the sky: the cumulus had a ring around it, another cloud approached, and they clashed—suddenly, amid the destruction, the sky took on form, events occurred (and then again, a little later, vast formlessness; a history of the clouds in the sky is inconceivable)

A woman who blossoms only when eating

Condemned to understand the language people speak when looking at shop windows: the sleaziness of the familiar

September 14

"If I don't go to bed with someone soon, I'll be completely lost, I won't know who I am any more"

The journalist on the phone: so coy, so flattering that it was very hard to answer him: I could think of no reply that wouldn't have struck him as "coy" (Not even silence was possible; the trap was perfect. Journalists should be silenced before they even open their mouths, they shouldn't be honored with so much as a word—but to such people that, too, would be coyness)

A man with merciless, expressionless eyes; he has to keep winking at people to give himself the semblance of an expression

Love can grow strong and serene when the forms are observed; otherwise, feeling gives way to sudden coldness

Art: life made majestic

My greatest achievement of late: accompanying the stupid remarks I sometimes make in a panic almost simultaneously with a kind of aside smile, which instantly transforms my panic into a wistfully mischievous gaiety

Fear of the seriousness that leads to wit; as though one were obliged to put up with seriousness until it turned to humor (see above)

"Once again a loathsome feeling of optimism spread within him"

An actress is sometimes said to be beautiful and nothing else; as though beauty were not an achievement in itself

The world moves me, yet I'm incapable of spontaneously helping anyone

I now have a strong, sure feeling and no need to say a word

Many of the young women here look as if they were working for real-estate agencies, as if their only conversation were sales talk

A story: two friends have been admiring each other's calmness for years; one day they discover that they have been imitating each other

While looking at clouds, fields, and people in the countryside: suddenly and with breathtaking clarity I see the history that has been going on down through the centuries hidden behind the menacing rumble of official history, the history of these people's sufferings, death, humiliation—true history, my history

Not to be neglected: how moved I am at the discovery of the button that someone else has discreetly sewn on—my feeling of wanting to be forever grateful

September 15

Morning: the child in bed seen as a beautiful line

Dream of dying: the feeling of death was a presentiment of the chill in the morgue

Memory of how I used to be: incapable of social life— whereas now I can face up to almost any gathering

If I didn't write, life would slip away from me

In the moment of wanting to love her, I bent over toward her and was really filled with love

At first I spoke formally, but when I noticed that I meant what I was saying, I cleared my throat and started all over again

All the telephone numbers in all the telephone books: where is there room for a life in all that?

He goes to the movies to drive the stupid look off his face

Clouds in the low, overcast sky, like shapeless objects under ice

In walking he teemed with wild, omnipotent thoughts, the substance of which he forgot the moment he stood still

Thinking that everyone wished for my death, I myself began to wish for my death

September 16

Envy: a state of desensitization; deprivation of all sensibility; unpleasant physical lightness, accompanied by pressure in the middle of the chest; incapacity for perception, assimilation, or concentration; notions of being ridiculous and badly dressed, of formlessness and at the same time of rigidity; of being insulted without insulters, of childishness, of seeing and hearing nothing; of being closed and masklike

A child who conceives a deep-seated revulsion for grownups from having to wait so often outside the toilet until a grownup has finished

Walking across the city. In the gaps left open by the masses of cars there are still a few isolated individuals, ashen pale or flushed, in incompatible states, and these people have subjected themselves to politics or world history, and amid the technological din they go around posing (like the figures shown in architectural drawings) at the foot of gigantic buildings, which are the essential while they are mere incidentals; moving through this catastrophe as through an underground hangar, I try to breathe everything in through my eyes, to preserve within me the forlornness of these people

A meal was placed in front of him in a way suggesting that many others had refused it

The music in this airport restaurant destroys all illusions with its dead, cackling cheerfulness; the people sit singly, glancing at one another now and then, but always at different times, and always with contempt; and so it goes back and forth in perpetual joylessness; people with faces, obviously divested of their stories or rather of the adventures for which they seemed destined, sit forlornly beside their attaché cases, stirring their coffee with controlled disgust, while raindrops tremble on the windowpanes

The big city lies in the midst of the countryside as though some enormous catastrophe had hurled its ruins haphazardly into a forest, and the rising mist makes it look as if all this had happened not so long ago

September 17

"I want you to go on living for many years." I was glad to hear her say that. It was a bright, pure, friendly night, reasonable through and through

During the lecture the serenely beautiful woman exchanged a knowing glance with someone, and then her features put on a dutiful grimace, a look of frantic glee that destroyed her face

Someone stepped up so close to me that I didn't recognize him

September 18

I managed not to ask her name

The woman wasn't smiling at me; she saw me and smiled to herself

Fatigue: one experience of *déjà-vu* after another

September 19

We looked at each other. When she suddenly turned away, I felt a cold shock

In my fatigue, all the voices I heard belonged to people I had known

September 20

The clutching of hands on the first day of school. Mother to weeping child: "Don't disgrace me. *Allons, en route!*"

After a brief "affair" she resumes her customary life: "I've found my rhythm again"

The leaves falling from the still shady trees glitter in the sunlight: my sense of being sheltered in the cycle of the seasons

Some motorcyclists howled past and I saw myself shooting them down from their machines. I was so pleased at the thought that I was able to look at the first young thug who came my way with a familiarity that surprised him

A. rubbed her eyes so hard to keep from crying on the first day of school that her cheeks are all inflamed

Someone who can't see *anything* without being upset

September 21

A., shaken with sobs, says from the bottom of her heart: "I don't want to go to *any* school"

Fingernails shining in the low-lying autumn sun

No traffic in this suburb, but even so there are cold people, disreputable weekend hotels, real-estate agents, massage parlors: dreary, dreary

How long the freshly fallen chestnuts keep cold in my hand!

A scolding is nothing to A.; words don't bother her, she says, only being pushed, grabbed, etc.

Sometimes a voice inside me, embodying what you might call my *impossible* self, speaks whole sentences full of hopeless gloom, just when my *possible* self is confident of a future

September 22

The dreariness of my present environment (a hotel) has led me once again, as it did long ago, to glowing dreams full of warmth and security

Why wouldn't I, even here, meet someone who has something in common with me?

The behavior of the rich (in France): courtiers without a court

The people here are as hostile as if they had no life of their own, and wanted none

The fatigue produced by small rooms

A. has come in for quite a few sermons about "asking for things." Now, when she sees something she wants in a store, she only hints with a little stage laugh, but she makes it loud enough for others to hear and interpret

The long bus ride through the suburbs today, past women who looked as if they had just been beaten, who in their beatenness had become briefly beautiful and above all vulnerable, stripped of their armor, their pretentious, forbidding look; who, thanks to the momentary loss of their surface lacquer, seemed to have become approachable. The defenseless gravity of these young women, who, once beaten, resign themselves to a life of suffering

September 23

The misery of school. On the way to school, A. practices a shallow-breathing exercise that is supposed to hold the tears back. In my inability to help her, I am close to fainting

I fled from time to the top of a tree

In the gray sky I perceive nothing—I need no signs, only something to perceive

Looking at the forlorn child: "Flesh of my flesh!"

A man with only one memory: he has stopped remembering for others

Now in my dejection, with my eyes that refuse to close, it seems to me that I have a "universal face" (but that if someone came to see this universal face I would be incapable of showing it, and would just sit here with my meaningless private face)

In the restaurant. Women at another table are talking about a friend who has died of cancer. They talk as rapidly and glibly as radio announcers, and with the same air of triumphant certainty

If observation is what you want, I believe I'm more observable than anyone else. "Don't look at me—I'm the boss!"

September 24

With arm outstretched as though in a fascist salute, a man strode to the doorway, rested his arm on the doorjamb, and stood there—instantly his gesture lost its meaning and became pacific

Advertisements for houses in artificial villages (*"domaines"*). The accompanying sketches show the latest conception of paradise: a father beaming from ear to ear as he strolls down a garden path with a child on his shoulders; slanting beach umbrellas; outside the house, slim young men arrange chairs for a party: "Here you will live from year's end to year's end as if you were on vacation" (none of the figures in these sketches has both feet on the ground—they are much too happy for that)

A child's hatred for the "outside" (the garden, the fresh air) that he is always being sent to: "It's so beautiful out. Why don't you play outside?"

All morning, flimsy thoughts have been running through my head, none that I can do anything with; nothing but prejudices, no surprises

Chestnuts at my feet in the warm sun: once again memory recapitulates fact, and once again I note that they do not coincide: "then" my experience of the fact was not harmonious and selfless as now, but slightly off; it was the experience of a man playing the part of someone gently kicking a chestnut in the warm autumn sun

The blurred photographs of dead people in the papers

A woman in the café. For a long time she sits quietly in the corner, then suddenly she starts breathing deeply and loudly

Doppelgänger experience: ". . . his specific way of thinking—his profoundly quiet way of letting his own life recede into the background and of bringing together the threads which originally ran at cross-purposes, and of introducing known threads into an unknown web" (Heimito von Doderer, *The Stairway at Strudlhof*)

I thought of someone who once, as we were standing on a history-saturated site in my native land, asked how I felt about the history of our country, and in my recollection of that moment (and of the hills converging in the mist) I felt as though a cellophane bag were being pulled over my head

D., whose mother had terminal cancer, said: "The poor old thing!" When I looked shocked, he said: "What do you want me to call her: 'my mother'?"

Sometimes, when someone is with me, we both feel that our relationship doesn't amount to much, and that makes us exaggeratedly attentive to each other

A. said: "It's a beautiful evening." Then, casting about for another reason beside the fact that there will be no school tomorrow, she saw the little bright clouds in the sky; she saw them because she will have the day off tomorrow (my guilt feelings at packing the child off to school day after day)

The lights of Paris at our feet do not spread out; they are viciously interlocked, entwined, enmeshed

September 25

Cool autumn morning, dark light, a feel of rain; still, the overcast sky seems illumined from below; against it, a cedar with foxlike branches

A. was friendly to me yesterday; she liked everything about me and defended me against other people's opinions

("Imprisoned in the tomb of his reality")

A.'s dread of school as of a cold foreign country (even in her sleep she seems to suffer)

Autumn storm: lightning flashes, not up in the sky, but in an avenue of trees down below; hardly any thunder, and no rain; only a louder rustling of the trees after the lightning flashes, which were not sudden but lit up slowly and could be followed into the distance

September 26

This morning, while contemplating a water tap (the functioning of which one takes so for granted), it occurred to me that the real anxieties, panics, desires experienced by primitive creatures have ceased to be anything more for people like me than models, diagrams, mechanical drawings, which are activated only rarely and on a very small scale, and are measured by the real panics, anxieties, etc., of *creatures*, regardless of what these "creatures" may be (the stupendous system of anxieties, torn out of their natural environment and injected into a limited, many-times reduced artificial environment such as our present Sunday-morning civilization with its water taps that function)

An idiotic worldly-wise grin on a sunburned face

These sudden malignant thunderbolts hurled at children in restaurants—after which the grownups, quite unruffled, go on with their fascinating conversation and the threatened child just sits there dozing (suddenly forefingers, fists, a jutting chin emerged from the conversation and were directed against the child as a last warning)

When I met the blond woman's glance, her eyelids fluttered, but so automatically that the movement repeated itself several times before she could stop it

This young girl has already learned to speak like a lady—entirely with the lips, and with no other facial movement

"Staring at people out of eyes full of indifference" (my early years)

Sunday afternoon: my rage against time; outwardly irritable, inwardly desperate

Sitting alone in a room, gradually feeling dirtier and dirtier

Extreme irritability after hearing a child's voice and nothing else all afternoon (how can I change?)

Spots of morning blue in the evening sky; on the darkening park terrace, the children flitting about silently, indistinctly, yet plainly visible

I've just noticed that the things on my desk, the paper with my notes, the scissors, the dictionary, the open volume of *The Stairway at Strudlhof*, the stamps, have a certain dignity that comforts me (". . . and now once again Melzer felt as if he had been unbound from the stake of his own ego . . .")

To caress a person's anxiety away once and for all

"He succeeded in thinking none of the thoughts that one ordinarily thinks; and here, without suspecting it, Melzer accomplished the second noteworthy intellectual feat of his life"

The bent back of a child, humped with misery; the yawn that replaced the suppressed sob; little dark clouds drifting across the sky like dead animals

Little boys outside a private school. There, I thought, stand the economic criminals of tomorrow

In the suburban train: contemplation of life's contradictions, appeasement of inner conflicts, of defenselessness in the face of school (praise of suburban trains)

Too tired to be human

Memory of certain harmonious states, when I was sure that everyone spoke my language and I was able to communicate with everyone; when people joyfully called one another's attention to every little perception: "Look, it's raining." What beautiful conversations

An unpleasant, unwanted monologue; I don't feel like talking to anybody, not even to myself

He didn't want to watch television (and didn't); but the thought that he *could* at that moment be watching television repelled him even more than actually doing it

Looking into the hotel kitchen from outside on a rainy night, I watched the dishwasher drying the knives, forks, and spoons and saw the virtuosity with which he slid them out of the towel into the right compartments. Once again, I placed this image in my future life and saw myself with a wreath of hair as thin as that of this elderly kitchen helper with his blue apron and his virtuosity at least in drying dishes

September 28

The wind in a dog's fur; the hair moves only on the surface
(memory of spring)

People on avenues of trees, in the shelter of avenues of trees,
walking on and on, sheltered from the rain, while leaves fall
before them and behind them; and now—so thin has the
foliage become—a shimmer of sunshine in the lower branches

My (slightly sadistic) hope that A. will never entirely get over
the forlorn feeling that makes her turn away from everyone

Relief: no matter how picturesque, how beautiful the sky is,
I have come to expect nothing from it, no solution, no diver-
sion

I mustn't let the unused rooms get spooky

How good I always look when I feel forsaken: how athletic,
how healthy! (A better man)

In the dark room the smell of a just extinguished candle

At least once a day I must succeed in wanting to *be* nothing
at all, just as Melzer succeeded in *thinking* none of what one
ordinarily thinks

September 29

After a hard night, I pass my dreams in review and get the
impression that I was in real physical danger at one point

Thunder this morning: at the end a hissing, then a rumbling,
very close; then again a long peal of thunder, which crosses
the whole sky, comes back, turns around! and after a long
while stops somewhere in the distance

Contentment: at a bus stop, sitting on a step with a child in
the warm sun, waiting

At a children's party in the garden with amiable, sophisticated, upper-middle-class women, who seem assured of winning the game of life. In such company I always get the same feeling of wanting to please but of doing everything wrong; I make unnecessary motions and force myself to be amiable to these strangers and their even stranger children, who sit on each other with expressionless hostility or play their games of war and violence. I thought I'd thrown off my feeling of belonging to a lower class, of being an upstart without a background, but here it is again

The teacher whose child died of leukemia. Throughout the years of the child's illness he prayed for him inwardly whenever there was a moment of silence in one of his classes

September 30

Gradual awakening from harmonious sleep: a rubber arrow, whose suction cup had fastened on the wall, slowly came loose and fell to the floor

In talking to people, someone starts saying something that he has often said to himself. Suddenly he breaks off and cries out: "What a silly thing to say! Lucky I see people now and then!"

A thrill of beauty on the desolate street beside the railroad embankment—and at the same time terrified that shots will be fired at me from that approaching car

In the middle of the night, lit by the street lamps, the bright, glittering leaves fall slowly from the trees; vision of the people who often stand still at night on the avenue, all showing the rigid, distorted faces of criminals; dead, brutal faces in this neat, elegant avenue of trees, more sharply delineated and more frightening than in the Métro, chiefly because they are set apart by the trees all around them and over them, and because of the way they stand still among the trees, rogues'-gallery-like; pictures of the Evil One, always in profile

October 1

Looking for thoughts to appease the painful pounding of my heart, I thought of women; the pounding continued, but ceased to be painful (an untroubled night)

The sturdy, lively, brown-haired woman in the Métro; all other faces became artificial—and already, as I watched her getting off, I thought of her as someone lost forever

Flowing through Métro passageways with the stream—how wonderfully sealed off we are: a conceivable way of life

Beware of people who keep telling you how helpless they are in money matters; maybe it's true, but as often as not, their feeble attempts to live up to their conception of a competent business person make them unpredictably ruthless, and possibly without knowing it they may defraud you more ruinously than a real businessman

Why can't I summon up any feeling for these afternoon figures in the café, sitting stiff and silent or standing stooped over the bar? Edward Hopper, for instance, might have given them a sad past, whereas I can't conceive of drawing them; all I see is blank faces

The sad Algerian bus driver, who gave up his job because he couldn't keep from crying when the passengers handed him tickets they had just been picking their teeth with

I think there are people I couldn't get interested in even if they had saved my life

It's true that he says clever things, but I keep forgetting their connection with him—so despite his cleverness I think of him as stupid

A flustered, hesitant property owner (a little later I met a resolute, self-possessed pauper)

October 2

Lay awake for some time, conscious of a certain spot in my back. When I dropped off to sleep, that spot figured in my dream, while the rest of my body was still awake; sleep began at that spot, and spread slowly and gently to the rest of my body

The bus driver spoke of his nervous breakdown as though relating the most usual of occurrences: *"J'ai fait ma dépression là-bas à Meudon-La-Forêt"* ("There is a house in New Orleans")

The arrival of the suburban train in the metropolis on a Saturday afternoon: young women, looking adventurously about, a man with a swollen nose, beside him a girl with the skin of the same feature peeling

It occurred to me that perhaps people who don't read don't know what they are doing, that it's impossible to get through to them

Forests (especially deciduous) in the vicinity of big cities: the most dismal, infernal, cannibalistic, nondescript spots in all Europe (with horseshoes nailed to the trees); they make you want to lip-fart instead of talking, to lie down on your belly and bleat. Kids running rampant with firecrackers; peevish-looking families out for a hike, slippery wet sludge underfoot, dog shit on uncovered tree roots, prickly chestnut husks, blackness before my eyes—and yet, from time to time in this unparalleled wasteland, this outsized mockery of a back yard, I glimpse the possibility of a forest, something that will unfold before my eyes and live up to "the word's promise"

October 3

Last night has made me believe in dreams again—not that they mean something or communicate something, but that they show us another, sublime world, which arches over the waking world. In this other world the characters of waking life reappear, but here at last they are free from the straitjacket of their history, elevated to an ideal space vibrant with eternity, where first is last, where the darkest night can be full of peaceful strollers and the brightest day can be deathly still, and far in the distance a single figure with a short head start over the atomic explosion, which proceeds to roll over the landscape like a dust cloud and wipe out first the runner and a moment later ourselves, the onlookers (still, the banal perceptions of the waking state are worth holding on to)

Polite conversation about literature with a stranger who didn't really want to know anything but only to ask questions at random. In our embarrassment we both kept rummaging in our pockets. Now and then he would cast a sidelong glance at his wife, who would stop nearby to listen and "participate," while I cast sidelong glances at nobody, prepared to break off the conversation at any moment, yet continuing to talk, explain, or occasionally express agreement. My body played no part at all in the proceedings. In the end it hung heavy, cold, and neglected on my exhausted larynx, and I'd rather have been that cold, cast-off body than this bored and toneless sound box

Conversation with a mathematician: he defines the *esprit mathématique* as, first, the ability to reverse every formulation—if one can say: "The glass is on the table," then why not: "The table is under the glass"?—and, secondly, as the ability to minimalize every series of operations; that is, to inquire what operation in a series we can omit without changing the result (his young son, he told me, already had this *esprit*: "Can the table stand on three legs? Or on two . . .?")

An image as I walk in the evening: the narrow little two-story house among others on the main artery. On the ground floor a young fellow is standing in the lighted open window; on the second floor, directly overhead, but behind Venetian blinds, stands another figure, smoking: deep Sunday-night gloom

At the restaurant. After repeated threats, mother approaches child, who holds up his hands to protect not his face but his head. Then, though forbidden to do so, he goes wandering around the room. Father steps in: "This isn't a playground!"

Child asks for peanuts. Father replies: "This isn't a circus!" Deep Sunday-night gloom

Drinking wine: *All of a sudden I have time*

"Head reeling with strangeness"

October 4

I use the first hour of waking to investigate myself in all directions

Sometimes, when the mathematician is not concentrating, his pupils dart up and down and side to side like the white spots in the tennis video games at the cafés

If only I can keep from being carried away by my own eloquence, I may get a good night's sleep

Late at night, in the middle of the conversation, a deep, gentle moan was heard; thinking it was a child, we stopped talking; actually it was the brakes of a truck in the distance

October 5

For a while last night the house owners listened to me almost devoutly, as though they were just finding out what a writer is. Embarrassing moments. The only thing I could do to help myself and them was to change the subject (to blue jeans, for instance)

The suburban train is waiting at the station—at the last minute a man comes running up the stairs, so excited that in getting on he almost loses track of his feet. Then another man comes along and takes the stairs at a leisurely pace as though this train were no concern of his, saunters down the platform, and then finally, with sudden decision, makes a dash for the train. At last the train pulls out, and all the passengers pass their hands over their frozen faces

Fantasy: my whole life is a treasure and I can acquire little bits of it by walking, moving, preparing myself for every little impulse

Grandmothers who sing in speaking to their grandchildren

While ironing, the girl sings the words of the song coming out of the radio ("You're sixteen, you're beautiful, and you're mine"); at the same time, the scraping and clicking of the iron and the smell of iron-warm cloth

The myth of Narcissus: doesn't it seem possible that the long, inquiring contemplation of one's own mirror image (and in an extended sense, of the things one has made) prepares and equips one for long, steady, penetrating contemplation of others? (The sterile, modern kind of narcissism strikes me as just the opposite: one stares at others, hysterically proclaiming one's interest in them, while disavowing one's own self)

"I'm so happy right now that I can't read"

Here in a foreign country I seem to have a dignity that I lack in Austria (here I am not a prisoner of my surroundings)

Even in a state of rest the child's wrists are as white as alabaster

The mathematician has been treating us to 8-mm. films of Senegal, where he works; all they show is people in bathing suits beside the water, in the water, on the water, or "the market" (of Dakar) . . . "it's so alive, not sterile like the markets here," or aquatic birds. Some home-movie makers seem to be interested only in leisure—dreariest leisure

October 6

A philosopher looked me in the eye and said: "Do you love France? I do not love Germany"

The children in most home movies seem to lose their personalities and cease to be anything more than "children in home movies"—engaging exclusively in children's occupations (games, swimming, splashing, bicycle riding . . .)

Progress: hearing the sounds of a fight, I kept on going, I didn't waste a glance

Occasionally, in the course of a day, time makes strange leaps, as though one had dozed off

Doing nothing in the darkening house this evening, I had the impression that I really "suffer" from time; absurd—I held my breath and felt invaded by suffering, not pain, but a persistent inner sickness. For the first time I was able to apply the word "suffer" to myself, thinking all the while that anyone I tried to describe it to would only say: "What's that again?" (The sensation of an old sewing machine moving slowly in my chest.) In that moment I discovered that the spells of malaise I had hitherto experienced were symptoms of permanent suffering; as though I were to say to myself one day: So now I'm really sick! (Absolute incapacity for speech) —And then A. comes along with her hands behind her back and says: "I'm glad to be alive. I'm happy about something but I don't know what. How awful if I were not alive!"

October 7

How often a conversation, which was free and natural at the start and, because this comes as such a surprise, warm as well, breaks off from one minute to the next, simply because I can no longer bring myself to respond to a perfectly simple remark and cast about frantically for possible replies—whereupon the conversation disintegrates into a dehumanized ritual of movements, words, etc., and perfect harmony gives way to a spasmodic jerking of eyeballs, heads, limbs—and speech as well

There comes a time when a child fighting with another, stronger child has only one weapon: a piercing, oft-repeated scream out of a perfectly immobile face—which invariably puts the other child to flight

Someone who from childhood on was deprived of open spaces to look out on or explore, who lived in a place where everything was inimically near and constantly getting nearer, would discover his only "prospect" in himself, in his body. This might be a (rather superficial) explanation for such a person's involvement with himself—the self as countryside—an involvement which would bring results rather similar to an actual trip around the world. One of this person's greatest adventures would be the "disengagement" of his body at a later phase, the separation of his perpetually crossed legs or arms, which are always compulsively clinging to some part of the body or supporting the head, until at last each part of the body stands by itself, untouched by any other, in perfect freedom and without affectation (the determination to achieve non-contact at all costs). After that, contact between the parts would again become possible, but would no longer be a clinging; it would be an incidental, secondary contact, something to take or leave, a passing by-product of free motion or rest

General strike today. Some stores still open, some buses still running, but now there seems to be no connection between people's activities and movements, only a loose, disjointed sequence, here a hesitant hammering, there the faint hum of cars starting up at a traffic light. The people seem lost without their work, they wander aimlessly, or take their children or dogs for an airing; there's noise on the boulevards, but a little less than usual, which makes for slight hallucinations, one might easily run into a car (but, to my surprise, there was the Eiffel Tower rising up from the strangely disembodied city: was I expecting the general strike to expunge it along with so many familiar landmarks?)

This afternoon, as happens now and then, a sudden release from time; gentle, blissful feeling of freedom, as if I had emerged from a tragic experience

Trying to talk a child out of the fear that I myself feel: "Look, there's so much fear in the world. So what do they need ours for? So let's just cut it out. There are so many bigger and more important fears." Rather fearfully, I talk and talk, but at least a short, sweet love springs up in the process

Night: a carpenter sawing and hammering in the house: what a wonderful feeling of security! ("Nobody minds work sounds!")

October 8

Trying to make myself think of something else: a painful, giddy feeling—better hang on to my foolish thoughts until "something else" turns up

Withered leaves blowing along in my wake as if they were pursuing me; on days of such clear, deep beauty, it seems as though no one could do any evil; as though such beauty must overpower *everyone* who encounters it, whoever he may be, whatever he may be plotting; peace through beauty; an old image rises up: the air has wings

"Wanting to go mad, she put on a wide skirt and went out into the street"

An unhappy person among people who couldn't care less: her breathing becomes a sighing

Sometimes I'd as soon commit murder as talk

Long time without fear: the guilt feelings that come of insubstantiality

Voices on TV: these thin, yet loud and brash voices: transcription of a stage play

October 9

A.'s uncontrolled sleep: body and face totally surrendered to sleep; at each exhalation her lips part slightly, her teeth sparkle, and a small bubble of saliva forms between them; the closer she is to waking, the more often these bubbles burst; her lips, swollen in sleep, part more and more; her eyebrows twitch and her lashes tremble

After a long night's sleep, several hours pass before—toward noon perhaps—my need to clutch at myself sets in: I must prolong this interval more and more (maybe a sleep cure would help me to get away from myself completely)

Cloudy fear—the eyes shouldn't allow it, shouldn't contribute, as it were, to this cloudy darkening; I must look attentively, with wide-open eyes—then the light will not be clouded by fear (resolutions while looking at a yellow, sunlit chair in the garden)

My first evening alone in the house: I pass the windows as often as possible, to make anyone looking in from outside think the house is full of people

October 10

The night must become my element!

"But it was her business to be satisfied—and certainly her temper to be happy . . ." (Jane Austen)

After spending the whole day with me, A., when at last a child arrived toward evening, became fidgety and helpless; later she said she didn't know how to play any more, she'd forgotten

A car drove past the house in the dead of night; brief feeling of satisfaction, as though we had finally been "hooked up"

I open a book written almost two hundred years ago, read a sentence, and suddenly imagine that I wrote it myself ("Silently they walked on—both deep in thought")

October 11

After months of being constantly with people and alone only when traveling: as usual, I'd forgotten how nervous, to put it mildly, it makes me to be alone. I feel as if my sense of hearing were dulled by day and sharpened by night; I tend to see ghosts both day and night—and besides, being alone makes me feel guilty; in spite of reading, looking at things, working, listening to music, I feel as I did in my student days that I'm doing nothing and experiencing nothing, just vegetating in lazy, stupid idleness

Dark, windy, comforting morning: doors and garden gates closing at intervals as people go off to work; a woman is scouring a pot on her front doorstep; a man, carrying his coat over his arm in his hurry to get to his car, is looking for something in his billfold; someone empties a plastic bag into the garbage pail and takes the bag back into the house; an elderly man in an open knitted vest steps out of his garden gate, looks to the right and left, and goes back in (after double-locking the gate); a young girl comes down the street, making rowing movements with her arms like an old woman; Keuschnig with his black attaché case, dark hair with a light streak in it, swinging his free arm as he walks, strides imperturably straight ahead; my mother appears in a poplin coat, holding her handbag in the crook of her elbow and a large shopping bag in the other hand, and takes a few steps with her ponderous behind. Gradually characters out of my real or invented past are walking down the suburban street this morning. And as I stand there with my face pressed against the windowpane, I feel like the family idiot, who spends the whole day staring at the street, at that stout woman now for instance, who is trying to run but only succeeds in making running motions with her arms and shoulders, while one of the supposedly running legs is at all times, as in walking, on the ground. The sky is dark and gray, but bright around the edges

The face of a young woman stepping into a department store first thing in the morning: "So amazingly fresh and undamaged"

October 12

Four hours of insomnia. Yield: two short sentences; then a pleasant black tiredness (as though in insomnia all actual worries were turned over and over, until each single worry, completely worn out, had found a quiet new place in my mind: salutary insomnia)

Someone on the phone: while saying goodbye he moves away from the mouthpiece

Longing for a place where it would be possible to take a walk without these howling dogs on all sides, jumping up on the fences in their eagerness to attack me

When the mother finally sees her child emerging from the school, her mouth opens in a hideous grimace of "joyful surprise"

We separated in the street and went our separate ways: as though going back to our real, anonymous lives

A step backward: in my new surroundings I've started running again when the phone rings (in the old apartment I'd progressed to the point of walking calmly)

In the kitchen, going through the motions of stirring a pot; the paralysis that comes over me when I find myself duplicating the desolate motions of a dead woman; then I feel as if I ought to stick my face in the pot

October 13

I had forgotten A. completely, and that woke me up; it seemed to me that a mere mask was lying there

As usual, she comes in, uses every pot in the kitchen to make something perfectly simple, burns the butter, then whatever it is she's cooking, until the whole house stinks from cellar to attic, and I can't get away from it. Then she has to rush off to one of her "meetings," leaving me to wash the burned and soot-covered pots and pans (which takes me a good hour) and wipe up the fat that has spattered all over the kitchen (finally, in writing, I manage to find these recurrent situations funny)

Experience of a housewife at the kitchen sink: for once she squeezes out her sponge less frequently than usual, but more slowly and thoroughly. Suddenly the squeezing is accompanied in her brain by music (musical fantasies; harmony, when daily motions are slowed down)

"J. was really persuaded that she talked as much as ever. But her mind was so busily engaged that she did not always know when she was silent" (Jane Austen)

So down in the mouth that even flies become welcome pets

D. kept laughing this morning on the phone; when I asked her why, she answered: "You see, I've already begun to work." She laughed because she felt disturbed

"My first run today"

October 14

Fantasy: an express train thundering through the suburban station; someone running ahead of it but refusing to scream

On the street today, the feeling that many people knew "who I am" but passed by without a thought of betraying me; some even tried to reassure me with a quick glance

The leaves racing over the ground; impression of a cavalcade, especially when I climb steps to reach the park where the leaves are blowing; there's one place where the leaves disperse in all directions, leaving a clean empty circle in the middle of the park

How much more domesticated I am, after all, when I'm talking to someone than when I'm roaming around alone! (Fantasy: unaware that I'm watching them, some people, including my calm friends, made almost unrecognizable by their adventurous loneliness, race through the cities of the world with wild, glaring eyes)

Toward midnight, objects, seen out of the corners of my eyes, are starting to crawl again

October 15

Just as I often do things absentmindedly, so I sometimes *think* absentmindedly (for the last year I have been trying so hard to pay *constant* attention to what is passing through my mind)

When I reproached him, he smiled disparagingly, as though the same reproach had come to him many times, not from others, but from himself

The sunlit stone wall in the morning: I try to perceive it *casually*, for fear of living a "beautiful moment," after which so many other moments would seem cold and hostile

The women running to catch the train held out their hands in such a well-bred way: thumb and forefinger joined, little finger upraised, as though holding a cup of tea (I was sitting on the platform reading, and the gale from a passing express ruffled the pages of my book)

Death of King Kong: and then his heart began to bleed

Someone who would stop in the middle of intercourse and say sincerely: "I really can't go on"

October 16

The woman with the big behind sat meditating in the living room; the children dared talk only in whispers; her husband was in the kitchen, washing the dishes

October 17

Frau F.'s cry of pain when I unceremoniously stuffed the shirts she had lovingly ironed into my plastic bag; her lament about the moth hole in a glove, as if nothing in the whole world could be more tragic; she has trouble getting her tongue around words, and they come out hopelessly garbled (so do mine, now and then)

In playing chess I noticed that I deliberately avoided looking at the piece I was threatening

The next day: the woman is squatting on the floor in deep-breathing meditation, the child is playing with piles of coins, the husband is in the bathroom washing the child's socks (to be continued)

Sitting alone at the table and looking out the window, I recovered the power of affection which I thought I had lost (the leaves on the tree are glistening as though they indeed were the last); reflection: if I were to die now, would I disappear completely—because I am not prepared for it?

October 18

As if not even dreams could surprise me any longer

How strangely the chess game began: neither of us really wanted to play, we picked up the men, hefted them in our hands, one tried a pawn opening, the other responded, and then we went on playing for two hours in the uncomfortable positions we had just happened to take when we noticed the board on the floor

Written with a ball-point on the plastic seat of the suburban train: "*J'ai lu barcarolles de Pablo Neruda coll. Gallimard/ Lisez-le, je vous en prie. C'est trop beau.*" And in the same train I looked at a woman I had once known, and thought: What a disgrace!

A precise story, full of feeling: the feeling lies in the precision of the telling, not in any description of feelings

I reproved the child in words that were really meant for the responsible adult (too cowardly to speak to him directly)

October 19

When, as sometimes happens, I lose my feeling for my own life, other people's way of life strikes me as a threat; their shameless definitions of reality recover their power to blackmail me

Went to the bakery with Herr F. to buy a cake; he said: "I'll pay for the cake. You're providing the tea" (this eternal matching of accounts among people who aren't quite friends)

I keep forgetting what I'm doing; I no sooner think of something than I forget it forever—but now and then I stop, follow myself back, and catch up with myself; that gives me strength

Listening to table conversations, as now for instance about Norway and "the Norwegians," I consider the possibility of never opening my mouth again, especially because in moments of embarrassment similar pronouncements escape me, and when that happens it's hard to go on living

A rare phenomenon: someone who, instead of falling into a sensual torpor after a big meal, seems to be invigorated and inspired

An old man with red face, dripping nose, and blue work trousers called out to a North African with broom and bucket on the other side of the tracks: "How goes it?" The other returned the question and, just as the train came rattling into the station between them, the old man replied: "I'm going to die soon." Then he pulled out a red-and-black-checked handkerchief and blew his nose so hard that his watering eyes stood out more than ever

When in a film a man of whom nothing is known stops to look at a woman, the viewer gets an instant impression of *déjà-vu* and knows just what to think. Of course he may be looking at the woman because he is lonely, but that can scarcely be made credible; at such moments a film has the commonplace eyes of a commonplace woman

Women's faces in the train: only the sex act is lacking to their beauty

Infuriated by the spectacle of a man looking high and low for a chair that doesn't creak, because he wants to write something. What, I wonder, will he write after this long, self-important search for a non-creaking chair? (Reminded of my disgust years ago when someone was trying to write a story in my house. Before starting, he solemnly littered my whole desk with strips of paper, on each one of which he had jotted a few words)

Brief feeling of warmth during the day when I know that a rare film or a football game will be shown on television that evening (even when, as usual, I have no intention of tuning in)

Children's program on TV; longing for the commercials!

When scolded or threatened by other aggression, A. automatically takes refuge in a book, just as I did as a child (instead of retreating into another room, or at least into a corner)

The lewd face of a gum-chewing blind man (the lewd part was the eyes)

One more *idée fixe*: what if, without wanting to, against my will, I should steal something in a shop? Today I very nearly walked off with an umbrella in a restaurant ("Everything that did not belong to him gave him physical pain; on the other hand, he despised all property")

Moments in which I am aware of all possible catastrophes but not troubled by them: a feeling of strange indifference; moments when I thumb my nose at death

October 20

Pleasant time of awakening. I thrash about amid the noise and confusion of dreams, pleasantly a part of them; my mind has not yet detached itself and is not yet able to think about them; it has not yet become a bare, cold point outside, a waking self, a mere fragment of the rich, warm, chaotic dream self (open the windows and the night mists escape in the form of a small fly)

I had no intention of saying a single word at the party, but on my way in I cleared my throat in spite of myself

Too often grownups had called the child with an air of urgency ("Come here, child, come quick!") and too often nothing of any account had happened. He no longer reacted to such calls

While looking for paper to write a letter to a friend, I thought: He's not my friend at all

How can I describe panic? Outwardly: all the nasty symptoms —sniffing the back of my hand, tearing my hair out, scratching, wiping grains of dust off the floor, inability to sit still; inwardly: distorted sense of distance in a city which has suddenly become enormous and where no help is available; feeling of deep night though it is still afternoon; *Schadenfreude* directed against myself: "Serves me right"; "feeling" of disgrace and guilt, but with no claim to tragedy. (Actually, panic is without feeling, only a big empty sore in the chest; no sadness, only the unfeeling certainty that even madness and suicide are beyond reach, that I will have to go on living after the catastrophe, in full awareness that there is no hope.) The other day, the face of a man trying to talk to a woman: its panic and confusion were similar to mine now, a twisted, hopeless smile

She has no feelings; what she calls her feelings are only her ideas of what feelings should be: she is full of ideas about feeling

My heartbeat rocks me as if I were a madman or a baby

October 21

In the early morning some people shuffle down the street as if they were wearing bedroom slippers

Yesterday, in my panic, I thought that to avert disaster I would have to sacrifice something, tear something up and throw it away, or cut my hair: "I almost cut my hair"—time and again I've thought of cutting off my hair, my vain vain hair (and now I remember going around frantically turning off radiators, because of an association of heat with decay—and at the same time I realized that I could never become a good socialist)

The grumpy old "fascist" passes the house while I'm washing the windows; now he can see that I'm doing useful work— but is window washing useful work in the eyes of a man like him? (When I said good morning, he smiled at me: the injustice of first impressions)

How do other people endure their daily guilt, their daily failures? All the faces I see show self-control

I used to feel relief on going out of doors; now I sometimes get the same effect while walking around the house

My sidelong glance at nothing, the look with which Ben in *Look Homeward, Angel* seemed, while listening to other people's nonsense, to say: Would you listen to that! But what I am trying to say when I put on that look is that "my angel" should listen to the rubbish that I myself have just unloaded in company: this sidelong glance at no one is a kind of plea for absolution

This day is so beautiful that I wish I could talk to no one, make the acquaintance of no one (heavenly conception of a gigantic, mathematically functioning city-state without government or administration, while the autumn sun shines into a bus in which we are all sitting together, neither knowing nor wanting to know anything of one another): "Let me, O Lord, breathe easy today—tomorrow, in any case, my feet will be cold again"

She tried to cajole me: "Your voice is so sad." But I remained indifferent

In one of his poems a writer suggested that I go to work in a filling station and learn what reality is: and indeed this author's biography (at least the one he writes about) is chock-full of these reality-cult occupations; maybe that's why his writing is as insipid as the story line of the movie *Three in a Filling Station*

At last: blissful deafness to all possible impressions

The dentist began every sentence with a word of endearment to comfort A. in advance

The timid wholesaler's representative in the pharmacy. After waiting in the background for some time (as though she had been a housewife too long), she finally came forward and said to the well-dressed pharmacist (black striped suit, dyed mustache): "I'd have spoken to you before, but I thought you were busy." The pharmacist, who had been standing there doing nothing, concerned only with the figure he was cutting, took a short step, not toward but away from the woman, and said: "I *am* busy." Apart from the two of them, no one was there but me, and I had already been waited on. As I was leaving, the pharmacist bade me goodbye most affably, as though to make the saleswoman aware of the difference between herself and a customer

Difficult: to be angry but keep one's self-control (perhaps it was possible only in old novels)

The moment the child falls asleep her cold feet get warm (and down in the street the sidewalk is drying in the night wind)

October 22

China: someday those who have disappeared will come back and tell their stories; and when that happens they will seem as alive as is possible only in those believed dead. Down with the news! And away with "travelers' " reports!

Ecstasy after hours of housework (perhaps from the steaming cloth under the iron)

Sometimes the spoken language, which has always been my medium, strikes me as so shatteringly true as to make it unthinkable that the people it unmasks will ever change; perhaps we need a constantly renewed, ever-changing spoken language (I don't mean a jargon or argot), not a single, eternally true, one might say biblical one; but it seems unlikely that any one person will be able to devise an eternally new spoken language

A man in a blue blazer is taking a child for a walk; he must be freshly unemployed, for he seems unused to walking with a child on a workday; he leans slightly back in walking, as though the world of leisure were not his element and were resisting him

Asked for a handout, I looked at other people in my embarrassment; then even more embarrassed at having taken refuge in others, I looked at my watch, etc.

A policeman suddenly bends down to pick up something a passerby has dropped: instant vision of the policeman overpowering and arresting somebody—just because of the surprising movement, unusual for a policeman

Lunch hour. One after another the girls come out of the office buildings and start down the street with short steps, trembling cheeks, and pinched-in behinds. But after a while, if the café or restaurant is not too near, their bodies unbend (at the sight of *one* with a different expression, or rather with an expression of any kind, I realize that I've been unjust to *all* of them)

Fantasy of a beautiful conversation in which all the thoughts I have had helter-skelter in various conversations with myself form a harmonious sequence and in which, by joining thought fragments that have hitherto been far apart, I am able to bring them to life for others and for myself as well. What bliss to be suddenly "gifted with speech," to recover something I had thought lost

Bank notes in my hand: once again I can't help imagining that I've stolen them

Loathsome words of praise: "hard-nosed realist"

Marionettelike movements in panic (seen in Hitchcock's *Blackmail*); and afterwards two women sit down across from me on the train, moving like robots or like policemen disguised as women

Friday evening in the big city: on every street corner, looking blankly into space, stands someone who is going to ask me for money / and everyone else I see might just as well be his accomplice / the bus takes a detour because the usual route is blocked by "*travaux*" / on the bus even the passengers who are used to the worst sigh and try to get off ahead of time (it can't be done, the door is closed) / whichever way I look, someone is shaking his head over someone / an old woman struggling to cross the street tries to catch my eye, as though needing an ally at least for that one second / she got her ally, and against the yellow sky the chaos, if nothing else, seemed monumental

An auto horn barely audible in the weekend din: touching that someone should still be trying to make a sign

October 23

My embarrassment when Frau F. referred to the room with a desk in it as my "workroom"; I immediately told her it was the "ironing room"

Frau F. said: "I'm not beautiful; I'm too ferocious." A. replied: "I wouldn't want to be gentle either, I'd rather be ferocious," and she showed the gap in her teeth

The sound of knocking from the hull of the sunken ferry turns out to be the sound of corpses rolling around inside the ship

She said: "I've stayed friends with all the men I've ever loved," and I thought: I won't let her do that to me!

The blank faces of the fascists. And they all seem to be wearing wigs, even the young ones; blankness masquerading as pride (pride in their absence of expression): they can't hope, can't have a vision of anything; I can't even conceive of them as *waiting*

G. is so distanced from herself that she has no difficulty in being permanently in love with herself; she finds it so easy to look at herself from a distance that she will never succeed in being severe with herself

Two children on the waiting train: *"Quelle heure est-il?"* — *"Cinq heures."* — *"L'heure de la mort"*

October 24

The clear, dark daylight yesterday; all the houses seemed "to be out of doors" (Karl Valentin)

Afternoon shopping: the streets were so crowded that the children had to walk step by step like grownups; if one of them tried to hop a little, someone would bellow him to order

Early in the evening I remembered that people were coming "to see me": deep kitchen depression as though embarking on a jail sentence; and then they came, and within two hours we had shot off every available commonplace. (My talisman was a small apple in my trouser pocket, the apple smell clung to my hand all evening.) Read the newspaper after they had left, and it crossed my mind that all these words had got onto the paper by the same process that makes alcohol-testing bags discolor when drunks breathe into them (Death: *Et in arcadia ego*"—Panofsky: "What was a threat has become a memory." —What became a memory is again a threat)

Looking out the window of a waiting train, I had ridden ahead in my thoughts; then the train started and soon overtook me: strange moment of duplication, when my thought ride and the train ride coincided, a kind of flare-up, and then there was only the train riding on

Sometimes, when I follow total strangers into a movie house, it seems to me that I am trotting after older relatives (but this fantasy never becomes a concrete memory)

Suddenly and for the first time the desire to live forever and also the feeling that I could bear it (just as the drizzle suddenly became a downpour, putting a jolt into the movements of the people on the square)

The crowd on Saturday night. Fleeing to the artificial light of the boulevards, they take disjointed postures and play dead; genre scenes staged with puppets, while in the wings civilization has already collapsed; at the center the interchangeable figure of a fire-eater; and no one in sight whom one might possibly trust

". . . a feeling of invigorating peace, which the clumsy guide spoiled with his pedantry, relating in detail how Hannibal had once fought a battle here . . . I reproved him sharply for his ill-advised evocation of long-departed ghosts . . . The least he could do was refrain from rousing the imagination from its peaceful dream with tumultuous echoes . . . Naturally I could not make him understand what feelings this mixture of past and present aroused in me" (Goethe, *Italian Journey*, April 4, 1787)

Actually, I think of death from morning to night almost without interruption, usually in a rather frivolous, offhand way, as though renewing some foolish bet with myself

Enemies: no more impulse to revile, fight, crush them—only the fear of their outliving me: the most shameful defeat of all

October 25

The starry firmament with all its constellations was very clear, but without presence, absent, without mystery; as though the earth were stronger, more powerful than the unstable heavens; the heavens conceived as a transient aspect of the earth, a passing cloud formation

"Do you understand me?" —I understand you, but understanding you turns my stomach

Motionless clouds, then a few start racing across the sky: vision of eschatological battles

"He chanced to look out the window and see . . ." (That would often apply to me)

He immersed himself in solitude to prepare for being with people

I must learn to look at people so serenely that they begin to move inside me (with most I have the feeling that they have been "cured too soon" and will therefore never know what it is "to be sent home")

Something worse than fear of the unknown: the fear of suddenly facing someone known

October 26

When someone decided to live alone for a while, people asked: "Why is he hiding?"

Sometimes I meddle in other people's futures with advice and encouragement: as though wishing to provide myself with substitutes for what I cannot develop in myself

While washing the windows, I heard applause in the street; but it was only children running past in sandals (the need for pleasant delusions at least once a day, to push *together* a little the happenings that are usually so dismally separate)

While they were praising me, I had the feeling that I should show them my profile

So many driving-school cars in the quiet suburbs

The evening of a deaf, subdued day, and still nothing has opened up: even if I had an illumination now—nothing could save this day ("Where is my soul today?" —And: "Perhaps this will give me beautiful dreams")

October 27

Transform the feeble melancholy of being-alone into a force for being-with-others ("High tension line, fall down on me!"— words from my daily rhetorical litany)

Rainy days when there's no way of telling whether the drops under the old women's eyes are tears or rain; and a child steps out of a house with his finger deep in his mouth, as if he had just been soundly scolded

I decided to abandon the goal, pursuit of which was making it impossible for me to do anything more than barely function; then at last, for the first time today, I felt that I was really alive; a delightful fantasy inspired me, and the world as well;

once again there was no difference; "the lights went on, the music began": the columns of people moving to and from the station ceased to be columns; at the post office stood potential friends, waiting peacefully for their phone calls: I had recovered my voice in the dusk, in the crowd (Fantasy through aimlessness, I thought)

"To be as I am"—as I am when I let myself go

Achievement: I have learned to leave a room nonchalantly (most of the time), oblivious to the looks of the people who stay behind

Instead of setting the empty garbage cans down in front of the garden gates, the garbage collectors threw them, as if to demonstrate contempt for the inhabitants

"The reality of guerrilla warfare" (collect more of these "reality" phrases)

October 28

Good that certain questions are no longer asked ("Have you seen such and such a movie?" etc.). I am often made idiotically speechless by my determination not to ask them

The brief contempt in the mother's face when the child didn't want to play with her but only look on; in that moment her features, usually so animated, took on the rigidity of a mask: as though a film had stopped for the barest instant and then gone on ("What a tedious child you are!")

Getting the evil eye from looking sideways

The repressed, hesitant, disembodied movements of a housewife, e.g., while folding a sheet (reconstitute the tragedy of the situation): "the reality of folding sheets"

Though I haven't taken any examinations for years, I have a sense of being examined while doing my everyday chores:

that is why I often find myself "boning up" on the most commonplace activities

The child was so hyperactive with boredom, and I was so tired, that the figures on the television screen moved as in a deep, deep room, deeper than the room we were in

October 29

Boredom as a feeling that one is leading the wrong life: a slight but real pain deep down in the chest, or rather a sensitive fringe along the rib ends—comes from thinking about a child's boredom, which is a horrible sight to behold if one has no remedy (is one to suggest a walk? or work?), and yet, might there not be a "triumph of the will" over these rapidly changing dictatorships of sensation? Suppose I were to try for a whole day to resist all changes of feeling and maintain a certainty (a certainty as such, without an object)

Learn, while working indoors, to keep looking out the window

I am able to perform certain manual activities, but I would be incapable of explaining how I go about them: I make unconscious movements which go wrong the moment I try to analyze them (with me no Taylorism is possible, I simply cannot rationalize myself; in all manual activities I just try to muddle through to a happy end)

Afternoon. Fantasy of running amok in the street. Unable to vent my rage on the person who had aroused it, fully aware that there was no possibility of doing or even saying anything to that person, I developed my running-amok fantasy, which was directed against my immediate surroundings. I wanted to plunge a knife into a woman I'd never before laid eyes on, I wanted to kick in a shop window; but at the same time, exhausted by the fantasies that were boiling up so hard inside me that it wouldn't have taken much to make me act on them, I felt a faintness, a weakness that drained me body and soul; in the end I made no other movement than to scratch the back of my head

The television journalist spoke of "internal difficulties"; I thought he was referring to problems with his station, but he meant that he was depressed

Proud that prostitutes have been speaking to me lately; they didn't use to (and I give them a friendly reply)—so I must have changed, after all (and dogs seem to like me better, too)

Unexpectedly a planned interview breaks loose and far exceeds the plan—making us a present of an evening and a conversation, nothing more

Sitting carefree at the window, seeing the lights go out on all sides, hearing the wind in the trees and no other sounds, seeing more and more infrequently the network of light cast by a passing car

October 30

I surprise myself in a monologue, describing the house I live in: "It's kind of messy, you know; the owners are North African Jews . . ." (I still know so little about myself)

Linguistic euphoria is needed for a poem (even a desolate one)

As I speak of myself and feel a pride in myself, I see the small, wind-buffeted fir tree in the autumnal gray outside the window: it embodies my pride and at the same time saves me from sentimentality

After a solitude which had indeed become hair-raising, which made his whole body tremble and his voice fail him, he boarded the train and (though cigarette smoke ordinarily repelled him) went straight into a stinking smokers' compartment, and there he immediately felt relieved; a short while before, he had just wanted to collapse and bleed to death

Outburst of madness over one little smudge too many, as over one little word too many

"I will not write another poem until I have a new view of life"

Peaceful night full of consciously endured fear, which, because it was conscious, never threatened to turn to panic; only at the moment of undressing, a feeling of defenselessness, a frantic anticipation of the assault

The thought that I was going mad was accompanied by the thought of the villagers and their malicious glee

A supermarket chain has tried to sell products without brand names; it didn't work; though cheaper, the products without brand names do not sell as well

National holiday at the Austrian Embassy: men in dark suits keep running their hands through their hair while listening to utterly vacuous speakers; the strange uninterrupted movement of hands rising to hair while someone is saying how homesick he is for Austria. —A French deputy boasted to me that he never read modern writers (twenty pages of Balzac and ten pages of Proust—that was his daily ration); modern writers, he said, knew nothing about the cares of the people, which were his stock-in-trade as a deputy (whereupon he listed the problems of the people, unknown to modern writers). When I asked him if he didn't think modern writers might be able to tell him something about the hitherto secret, never before expressed cares of the people, he told me how he had recently amused himself figuring out how much time he devoted to his political petitioners: an average of twenty minutes per specimen of the "people" he represented—that sufficed to keep him informed about the cares of his constituents; with this remark, which seemed to strike him as a suitable brush-off—he had caught sight of a fellow politician and motioned to him—he tapped me on the shoulder as though he had said everything one can say to the likes of me, made a square-lipped smile, and went on "mingling" with the crowd (face uplifted in an expression of permanent benevolence)

I recovered my sense of humor when someone told me something I hadn't known about myself (I myself am my phantom-enemy—and this monster must die; perhaps in some of my fears I am only a victim of the yellow press)

This evening reread passages from the Bible, then saw *Young Mr. Lincoln* again: shaken out of my daily perplexities, but these are not eliminated or thrust aside, rather they are made to shine as something that can and must be borne (Hagar, who, when she thought her child would die of thirst—they had been sent out into the desert—did not go away, but "sat over against him"; and Henry Fonda's Abraham Lincoln, with his bodily movements as calm and clear as letters from another Bible); I had to take a deep breath to keep from crying

November

At the same place where the moon was shining early yesterday evening the sun is a spot behind the clouds, without beams, without radiance; dark, earthly, unghostly morning—keep it that way!

Noticed that to take in the most ordinary (especially the most ordinary) images on TV, I have to concentrate as much as in reading complicated sentences in a book (though, in the case of TV, to no purpose)

The people who take the bus in the morning whistle the tunes from last night's television programs

Nature in the city: at least it doesn't *luxuriate* (Austria: luxuriant nature); here the main nature (and nature enough) is the sky

Question addressed to a housewife: "What do you see when someone says 'apple tart'?" — The housewife: "Crumbs on the floor"

With what exaggeratedly masculine vigor men often perform actions that are usually performed by women, kitchen movements, for instance, such as throwing scraps in the garbage: they avoid bending at the waist or knees, which might look feminine (and that is why in so many of these movements they miss their aim, as in my own case, for instance, when, instead of hanging a dish towel on the hook, I tried to toss it briskly from a distance and missed); or in order to dissociate themselves from such activities, they (or I) perform them with their feet rather than their hands

As I enter the waiting room, the automatic word combination: "unheated waiting room"

Gradually the certainty of being able to invent (the kind of power "that oppresses no one")

Looking at a woman, the thought that I would be forever secure if I were beautiful

Evening. Out of doors. With a child. Down below, the city, glittering. Once again the queasy feeling of being a hero

The one thing I haven't done with my obsessions is to make myths of them: "Under the protection of my myth" — "In the insecurity of my obsession"

The gentle sounds of a midnight film; the chalked outline of a murder victim on the sidewalk; and suddenly the autumn leaves blow over it

Presidential elections: the experts frown; even I feel a weight on my chest, as if something were at stake

Careful not to acquire any pet phrases

Disgruntled—because I was unable to think

"Why are you making such a face?" — "That's the way I look when I'm buttoning my coat." And then a woman in the crowd gave me a tender look

The sounds in the house—little by little I must learn to recognize where each one comes from; and shake my head reassuringly when visitors look up in alarm

On certain rare days I am favored with an unlimited, all-embracing awareness: capable at the same time of daydreaming, of remembering, and of apprehending the world around me in full clarity, each of these faculties reinforcing the clarity and intensity of the others

Certain activities make me feel so secure that if the Monster of the Universe were to step in now he couldn't hurt me (and wouldn't want to)

My past: when something was good, I remember the situation; when something was bad, I remember my part in it

The old woman was running to catch the waiting train: because her legs couldn't move any faster, her face, especially her mouth, was hurrying like mad

I'll sleep well tonight—I've done nothing but listen all day

When looking around, when glancing over my shoulder, I must nevertheless keep a human face (a child can do it)

G.'s beauty is marred by the conspicuousness of her dress; one notices at a glance that her clothes are beautiful

Literature: discover localities that have not yet been claimed by meaning

Now at last, in the evening, comes an image of the day's misery; salvation

A voice like an accomplished fact

Today the leaves are falling faster than before (they have grown harder and drier)

"At sea, May 12, 1787 . . . I did not let these truly seasick thoughts of a man buffeted this way and that on the waves of life gain the upper hand" (but *how* did he stop them?)

The three children are friends—they are like a single ideal child; even their bodies are sometimes inseparable, making noises only to show or imitate one another, hugging one another, screaming and yelling in perfect contentment (also creating perfect contentment in the onlooker)

For a while an express train runs along beside the suburban local: behind the steamed-up windows sit people who have been traveling for many hours; they've come from the seashore

Absurdity: I suddenly find myself in a drawing room with upper-class ladies well versed in all the social frills: one of them is preparing an *oeuf à la polonaise*; as I look on, an unsuspecting child enters my field of vision; the woman draws the child toward her with a show of affection, but in reality she is moving her aside to give me an unobstructed view of her manipulations; later, in the salon, my silent amusement at the thought of how I of all people had got into such company; a trifling everyday tragedy accompanied by joyless laughter; vision of myself farting into their conversation; when at last I leave the house, the first thing I do is pee on the doorpost

My obsessions may be my private affair; but what actually distinguishes the obsessions of individuals from the myths of the many? — Thus far, no one has devised a language for translating the obsessions of individuals into collective myths; particulars dereified as symptoms of disease are not yet regarded as a new way of life; and besides, our daily obsessions lack the element of adventure that might make them into myths. Consequently, (a) we must try to find another language for our obsessions, and (b) make up adventure stories to go with them

The sound of leaves falling in the night—like dogs running, stopping, then running on

By the pattern of the floor tiles, a child recognizes a place where she was once made to go against her will

Entertaining friends in her salon, Madame S. began telling stories instead of merely expressing opinions as usual: in her this produced the effect of letting herself go

An officer on the train: unrecognizable waxen face, already prepared for burial

Someone whose mouth waters while reading the instructions on a package—on a Meccano set, for instance

"I would like to tape an interview with you, for educational purposes." — "Are you a teacher?" — "No, but I would first converse with some teachers and then ask you a few questions from the student's point of view"

"Where did you spend your vacation?" — "I didn't take a vacation, I worked." — "Oh, I, too, spent my whole vacation working"

A day without disturbance, without metaphysical complaints: an overstuffed day

A mouth still gently closed by the aftereffects of weeping, a calm face

The student went to the university in the morning with the flu; there he ran into some fascist thugs and had to take the back entrance to get away from them; when he came home that night, he was in the best of spirits and his flu was gone

Another Doppelgänger: the child in the school yard yesterday with the protruding occiput, small somber eyes and fat cheeks, in short trousers and tennis shoes despite the cold; I watched him with rapt attention, standing with a small group, absent and then all of a sudden wholly present, tyrannically ordering the others around, the sleeves of his sweater pulled over his hands (fulfillment and warmth in watching him, "as if this were it," and then I disappeared alone)

For the past year: "I don't have to play a role any more"

Dreams in which I am as petty as when awake

Listening to the journalist: his talk seems to have drained me of life-feeling to the point of utter emptiness; why? because he kept talking about "life-feeling"

The impassive faces of the engine drivers flashing through the station in their express trains; but then comes a train that slows down and stops, and the engine driver yawns (inconceivable in the ones that race through)

A worker who stands still, looking at something: caught myself thinking that he must be pissing (as though a worker couldn't possibly just look at something)

Dreams as aesthetic achievement: why couldn't one take pride in a dream as in a work of art?

After a miserably speechless day (my staring eyeballs saw nothing but surfaces without depth), I finally found a possibility of comparison and called it a thought (up until then, even the child had been only a mournful sound)

The telephone operator, when I called to reserve a hotel room: "*Êtes-vous une societé?*" — "*Non, au contraire*" (meanwhile, an American looked out the window and said: "What a gloomy weekend")

Triumph at the thought that I've found an idea and am proceeding to live accordingly

Looking out the window, an experience of beauty, yet unable (and unwilling) to say what is so beautiful out there and why: beauty as a removal of limits, an experience of unexpected openness

An old idea which gradually takes on body: that "if my murderer should come up the stairs," I would welcome him as a friend

I remembered the old saw about "a man's whole life passing before his eyes in the moment of death"—and it occurred to me that I could get that effect any time I pleased

In half-sleep I never, as in dreams, get images of something known, something actually seen; rather, I get a majestic silent movie composed of neomythical images

Standing in the suburban train, under the neon light, I lift my head and the light takes hold of me, frees me from the breech presentation in which I once again find myself in anticipation of the dark, menacing loneliness that awaits me at the end of this train ride—and in this feeling of security, "sheltered by the neon tube," I long to take a bite out of its glass so as to carry its comfort with me into my pitch-black isolation

Thought on entering the kitchen: perhaps in return for my accumulated kitchen work all will be forgiven me; perhaps all *has been* forgiven

Writing: safe again

In her memoirs an actress speaks with pride of a conversation with the powerful: "And I can assure you that they listened to us"

Learn from history: what a hoax! Nothing can be learned but short-term tactics

So far, my only idea of "the people" has been picked up in country churchyards

Herr F.'s mode of communication is so extroverted that if his interlocutor actually responds, Herr F. soon runs out of words and can only submit, helpless and perplexed, to the other's flood of talk

One woman indignantly about another: "She looks at me like a man"

Related: boredom, fear, aimlessness ("I'm so bored I can only walk in circles")

"How long have you been here?" — "A lo-o-ong time" (This "lo-o-ong" is sung by a child. It's very long)

A day spent without noticing others: after such a day I deserved to be afraid

Read a beautiful letter and felt that the "cordially" really came from the heart

Feeling of inferiority toward a man with illusions—they make him look so beautiful

She spoke desperately, staring at the fire, and I expected her to plunge into it to purge her desperation of its rhetoric

Looking at the constellations: why do we stick to the names that other people have given them; names which, moreover, diminish and delimit our view of them? (The same can be said of all name-giving in nature)

Frau F.'s face, malignant because of her inability to think and her need to give "tit for tat" all the same. When her husband reproves her for something, she, without even considering his reproof, reproves him for something else; the disorder on his desk, for instance

When someone makes a stupid remark—suddenly, in listening, I seem to take form, a motionless, larger-than-life form, and the objects around us seem to move abruptly, dissociating themselves from this stupid person, who becomes a formless something, a vague blob in this suddenly organized space

How often I recognize myself in newspaper photos of murderers!

I'm on my way to meet someone; but when I get to our meeting place I feel so far ahead of him because of my long walk that we can't make contact and have nothing more to say

A certain person is always curious and nothing more—that's why he knows so little

Evening shopping in the neighborhood stores: it warms me, even if I've said nothing but the names of things I wanted and a few words of greeting

The moment when the congealed world stirs with the last leaves on the trees and draws me into it; after that, nothing can happen to me for the rest of the day

The woman who has invited me to tea looks at me with flashing eyes. "I must tell you," she says, "that I am a Caucasian." — "?" — "In the Caucasus, you see, they never strain the tea." Whereupon she pours the tea into my cup, leaves and all

A whole day passed without fear (and without my combating fear by thinking it away, thinking it through, etc.). And then the thought (no, the experience) that with such a day I have not "earned a peaceful night"; the fear which I had put off for so long went into my chest and became a full pig's bladder, which was being squeezed from all sides

A small, heavy object: marvelously heavy (a large, light object: marvelously light)

In sadness, the need to be attractively dressed

Carry a feeling through the crush in the Métro and take it home unharmed

When I come out of the movies, the people in the street are all the wrong people

No taxi now! The Métro! the bus! I need to think

I'm not a "pantheist"—but sometimes I manage to draw a pantheistic breath (against death)

At the movies: a man touched Raquel Welch's bare shoulder, and I became aware of my cold hands

Loss of feeling from too much thinking about death (a fascist trait)

Sometimes talking is so repellent to me that just to finish a sentence I have to raise my shoulders and brace myself

A chief of state has allowed one murderer to be executed and pardoned another. That compromises him as thoroughly as if he had let them both be executed. Now at least I'll never have to think of him again

In the end we spoke well, because by then it was only the speaking that counted, not ourselves, the speakers

Suddenly, in only a few sentences, F. disclosed all the classical symptoms of schizophrenia (persecution mania, loss of contact with the environment, etc.). It came as a tragic shock to me. Here was someone going to pieces before my eyes and there was nothing I could do about it. It was as if, from one moment to the next, she had removed to a place to which no one could follow her and from which she would never return

My moviegoing has become a disease: almost every film leaves me in a state of lethargy and hopelessness, with a kind of hangover that makes me feel as if I myself and all the people around me were living corpses (crawling away with dangling heads)—yet the next day I get restless again when my "movie hour" approaches

For the first time in years, instead of my old boredom I feel something slightly different and more impulsive: an aimless impatience

So thoroughly prepared for come-what-may that sometimes I'm not prepared for anyone

My special gift: extreme distraction, followed by extreme concentration

Two relentlessly tongue-wagging women with the cold eyes of bishops

A child sitting there with the composure of a physicist

Telling someone how I feel strikes me as a repeat performance, since I've already told myself

Back to the social gestures after long being alone: standing with a friend in the railway station, looking at the usual sights, which in my solitude always revived me and straightened me out, I felt obliterated by my friend's presence beside me, like an empty space in a place I had formerly occupied

"You want to know what poetry is? Just look at this." Whereupon I picked up my coat and took a long loaf of bread out of the deep pocket

The only feeling that really proves one is alive: the feeling of *unio mystica*

He stopped masturbating: suddenly his longing interfered

In the café—one look at the waiter gave me the feeling that he knew all about me

I saw an ugly woman and looked at her reproachfully

Achieve self-awareness not in anger, not in aggression, nor yet in humility, etc., but in serenity; self-awareness in serenity

Gentleness: energy made self-aware

December

Purest, strongest feeling = consciousness of death (my "consciousness of reality": consciousness of imminent death)

Suicide: the short story of my fear

After the catastrophe: learning to speak again

Love: feeling for another's gestalt

The catastrophe of being alone, made acute by a missing button on the child's coat

Need for philosophy

Standing so close to the window in your anxiety that you steam up the panes

In the last few days it has cost me extreme exertion to get a few words out (no, not to get them out, to *make* them); A. noticed this and sometimes took me by the hand, as though she didn't, as usual, need my hand, but I hers; no one has ever described what it is to be alone

Attempts to pull myself out of the swamp—as though this swamp (and occasionally the world of miracles) were my actual habitat and as though there were nothing outside it but the deadly mechanics of opinions

By now, at least, I've shot a few problems dead

I think of my eyes, and the station appears—sights appear

For the first time in this house, I've experienced fearlessness, not as absence of fear but as strength

G. has the abrupt movements of a child, though he is almost fifty; you have him in front of you and a moment later he frightens you by turning up behind you; his voice, too, is usually as ruthless as a child's, loud, demanding, importunate; when masturbating, he never thought of anyone but himself, being whipped; that was his stimulus

More and more often, even in times of utter listlessness, another voice seems to rise up in me, which wants something new and cries aloud and initiates this new thing with no help from me, and from this voice I derive an eagerness for the new existence that is building up (without the old me)

If at the moment of waking I could only look forward to the day without first having to plan it out!

Sometimes I take pleasure in everything, even idiotic activities like brushing my teeth

I have come to feel that almost any meeting with anyone is a kind of test, and the moment it's over I'm inclined to forget it, even if it has been pleasant, just as one immediately forgets examinations

Feeling of duplication at times of extreme fatigue, a kind of jolt away from myself (mug shot of my face when tired)

Watching the tongues of flame in the fireplace, vision of a church choir singing

She started talking with her usual vivacity; I listened without a word, waiting for her to burst into tears as usual (and in the end she did)

Moved at the sight of an empty bus, coursing bravely through an out-of-the-way street so early in the morning: the state as kindly provider!

Coming out of one shop and heading for the next on a bustling Sunday morning, surprised to catch my inner voice saying: "Actually, I'm a happy man"

Asked to repeat a certain gesture, someone recaptures his whole past life

Reading the classified ads in suburban papers ("Stamp collection for sale"; "Home bar for sale"), one is drawn into these people's dejection

Herr F.: "My wife can tell right away when I'm not thinking of her"

Rain on the roof like birds hopping about

Two children fighting—with the malignant gestures of their ancestors

A leaflet is put into my hand. "Broad masses," "farm and factory," "every town and village"—I read and lose all hope

I hadn't decided yet whether she was beautiful or not, when a beautiful woman stepped into the room

A man who has had many love affairs, but always one at a time: maybe it's just a matter of morality and optimism

Security guard at the airport: "Is that a book in your coat pocket?" — "Yes." — "I don't mind reading a book at Christmastime myself"

Sometimes, on a cold, frozen day, an accidental glance (in a supermarket) is enough to make everything "right" again, if only for a few seconds; as if it were starting to snow

January

Could it be that physical beauty implies a certain—if only a little—athletic vigor?

The corners of her mouth, split from eating apples (such big apples)

In a mute act of solidarity, walked a long way behind a raving madwoman; if she were to turn around and see me, she would fall silent for a moment

Man to woman: "Does sex mean so much to you?" — Woman: "Words alone aren't soothing enough"

The sagging shoulders and arms of amateur actors

The sound of the rain—like a box of matches being shaken

A day on which I have neither heard, seen, nor smelled my body: no sense of privation

Perhaps it was so easy for Brecht to assimilate and be influenced by political news because the medium through which he received it, the radio, was still a mere medium and not yet a self-sufficient fetish for "reality" (more and more often it seems to me that the news world—by decreeing that *worse things* are happening all over—destroys people's awareness of their own lives)

Anxiety: not a state, but an incessant, unbearable happening

After resisting the temptation to say something about somebody—a sense of strength and harmony

Discharged from all systems: in such unemployment the era of consciousness would set in (it was preceded by the—equally dangerous—era of being, for which, however, we feel no regrets)

Many footprints in the light snow (single flakes are still discernible): as of people running

And so my personal life merges with the universal and takes to its bed with wounds envenomed by television

A Palestinian leader on television speaking Arabic very calmly, while the interpreter translates into French with great passion

Perhaps I am gradually turning into the man of a new age, calm in waking, calm in sleep, and calm in death

It looks as if I'm able to think only when I'm involved in something

The Shah on TV. The thought that this is my enemy, who is insolently trying to outlive me, so that my death will at the same time be my disgrace. For someone like him, I might just as well be dead—as if I had to kill him in order to face up to myself

I thought of art as a parachute that would save me from falling

As though in the past year I had led several complete, more or less successful lives

Down with memory! I want life to be beautiful *now*, not only in retrospect

In the photograph I still looked like someone "who'll never make it"

My daily panic-fantasies are so devastating that I end by having to mumble to myself: The train is still running, the house is still standing, the child is still living, the deep soft armchair hasn't swallowed me up

Near the station: a middle-aged woman with a suitcase passed slowly by, looking very sad, and I thought: So the long trip was no help

People used to say that the blessed "would see heaven"; my wish would be to see the earth forever

The feeling (thought, fancy, realization, all together) that nowadays, at a time when so much is allowed, possible, etc., in the field of action, we (I, in any case) are subject to all the more interdictions, cowardices, etc., in the realm of thought (and this is why so little can be done in art)

Looking fearlessly down at the street at night—how much closer everything seems!

Liberation: when I no longer feel tacitly called upon to discover so-called scientific laws in everything I see

G. said: "One can only be attentive to others if one knows one is sexually up to the mark"

The clouds outside the window passed into me and became strange formations. I was in an ideal landscape, which was also unknown, stranger than the Arctic, almost colorless, but I perceived colors, and in the sky chunks of ice passed by instead of clouds; to prove this to someone who doubted me, I reached into the air and took one of the low-flying blocks of ice out of the procession; the ice grew soft in my hand, a pleasant feeling

The murderer who has not understood what he has done wants to avenge himself on fate (a different idea of revenge)

My kind of power: I bring down the shutter of my eyelids and capture all the people coming toward me

Take up philosophy with the thought: Let's see if it drives the fear out of me

"The odd thing about thinking is that apart from itself it likes best to think of what it can think of endlessly" (Friedrich Schlegel, *Lucinde*)

I said to G. on leave-taking: "My best to your children and [here I stood on tiptoe] to your wife"

Such silly remarks in books that move me: ". . . human beings must love something . . ." (*Jane Eyre*)

The euphemism "history"; perhaps if I were to learn, as completely as possible, the history of Job's reactions, this knowledge would shelter me and gather me into this same history: to become one after many? to be one before many others?

"It upsets me when you take notes in my presence." — "You must try to trust me"

Intense but imprecise memory? Then try a poem!

The epitome of beauty: if I say to myself *spontaneously:* "That was beautiful!"

"The idea of the 'I' must be regarded as the inner light of all ideas"

The face of the man on the train today. While unobserving, hostile to all observation, I let it move away from me, it came closer and closer, and gradually became the universal face, embodying man and woman in one, the face in a film episode whose climax it represented, deep and infinitely remote. I contemplated it with suspicion despite its remoteness—and as though the man had noticed all this, he shifted his position and looked in a different direction (his face had been that of a great actor, looming large even at a distance)

He looked at her in silence until at last she believed his life

Chessmen pushed out of their squares and crowded into the middle of the board—a human picture

On my way to bed, a small peeled tangerine in my fist, dry but elastic; erotic thought of a small, pretty woman, ready for anything

Sleepless in the night silence; then at last a sound, but instead of startling me, it jolts me to sleep for a moment

Street in total night: as though expecting tanks, deserted by all its inhabitants, fallow land, brackish water in the eaves

Feeling of health for some days now; "January cheer"

Encourage a child's feeling of sympathy, even for King Kong; most children are so hardhearted

I have never been able to reconstruct someone else's (Walter Benjamin's, for instance) thought; at best, with luck, I can gain an intense intuition of it (my kind of thinking is largely dependent on luck)

The old man in the shop today, who wanted to buy salt. They were out of the small-size box he usually bought, so he took a large one, remarking that the small box had lasted him three years. Eerie silence in the shop. Everyone realized that the old man had just bought his last box of salt

Connection between clumsiness and lack of control (inability to control objects)

But I have learned this much from Benjamin: that it is not possible to act as if one "did not think" (that poetry, at least in its beginnings, cannot escape thought, any more than Marianne in Ödön von Horváth's *Tales from the Vienna Woods* can "escape" the butcher's love)

The gaping jaws of my notebook

Flight from the incoherent day into trusty sexual fantasies, in which everything hung together

The feeling that I shall never again be bored (my counting mania—a symptom of boredom—has left me)

Again, at long last, I experienced love as a pain which suspends a lesser, commonplace pain

A woman on an advertising poster knitting: she gives me the liberating feeling that there's no need for me to know how to do anything. I've ceased to regard my lack of skills as a failing; why should I know how to do things?

Suddenly her eyes went rigid from repressing a yawn ("I yawn with my eyes")

The file of parked cars at night, their black rear windows: a funeral procession without a funeral

The couple go out because they want to talk to each other (they aren't able to at home)

I talked too much yesterday, saw too many people. My dreams at night were hectic and blurred

The worst thing the young girl can accuse anyone of is irony; she rejects irony because she knows more and wants more than she can say

Even if I were accused unjustly of the most absurd and hideous action, I could deny it only halfheartedly—because such actions have always been possible in my thoughts

The chopped-off past, which even now, "at sunset" (afterwards the dead snakes stop moving), raises its irrelevant head to frighten me again with its immensity

In my fatigue, contempt for all liquids, nausea even at the thought of appetizing ones

"It would disgust me to be amiable by you people's standards"

An aftersound like an afterimage (the ticking of an alarm clock that has stopped ticking)

The international feature writer. He stuttered, not in syllables but in whole words, an artificial stutter. When he wasn't talking, he was wheezing. His affability and enthusiasm seemed a mask for contempt, venom, hate. He made a big show of hurt feelings when I couldn't bring myself to call him by his first name (as customary in his country), and from then on he addressed me as "My dear sir." He couldn't keep still for half a second; when I had to leave the table, to do something in the kitchen for instance, he would call after me or follow me, and keep right on talking. A., who as usual when I have a visitor, especially someone she doesn't know, kept interrupting, was in turn—something that had never happened before —constantly being interrupted. When I reproved her for interrupting, I really meant the feature writer; the sighs I addressed to her were really meant for him. He knew every writer in the world, they were all his protégés. ("Beckett is looking a lot better than he was five years ago." — "I got my taste for oysters from Ionesco.") In leaving, after once again addressing me with murderous hatred as "My dear sir," he slammed the garden gate. I had visions of his coming right back, barging into the house, and asking me to "give back the trust" he had placed in me, so I locked the door at once. He rather made me think of a raving, disappointed suitor; in the end, he wasn't sure whether he'd write about me or not. He smelled of the lozenges he kept sucking (as a substitute for constant chain smoking). He was a spoiled (by himself as well as others) high priest of culture. His special trick was letting on that the obsessions of his interviewee (in this case mine) had always been his own, and he would piece details together with the dexterity of a pickpocket (His speaking voice didn't seem to belong to him; it issued alien and disembodied from his mouth; but when, as sometimes happened for a few moments, it became grave, heavy, and his own, it seemed affected and hypocritical. The same with his eyes; they would suddenly stare at me, but he wasn't really looking at me, it was just another trick, a pretense. I have to admit that he occasionally seemed lost and then he was almost lovable)

For a moment the thought of her condensed into a vision of love: the vision of the line of her cheeks

"How will you solve the problem?" — "Why ask me? Can you suggest anything?"

The danger of being so accepted by someone that no matter how badly one has behaved, one can always say to this person: "You know how I am"

Rare occurrence: while reading a newspaper story, come across a sentence that makes one look for the name of the person who wrote it

The child murderer, with whom I somehow identify, has not, as generally expected, been sentenced to death: on hearing the news, a moment of disappointment, as though he had been cheated out of his story

From an old English novel: "The appearance of a housemaid prevented any further conversation"

The rain sounds as if the drops were being caught in tin buckets; no longer coming down, but being hurled, this rain has suddenly made me think of a language: the language of the rain

A functioning house in the middle of the night: spooky

After a long pause a last raindrop, like a trailing bicycle racer; and then the only sign of rain is the sound of the cars on the wet street: "It was raining"

Someone who talks only in his sleep

Word for the state I have been in for some time: "Relieved." Certainly not happy or contented

Form: a product of (long)experience

Emerging from myself, I become a disembodied cosmic being, a virtual world, an immaterial, dynamic whirring

First sign of returning sleep after long wakefulness: eyes closed, I see things joined, which in my long wakeful thoughts I had gradually moved together; they have coupled with a soft jolt

In half-sleep my thoughts suddenly turned into a coffeepot

In paralyzingly serious moments I should always keep a balloon handy, to waft me out of my paralysis

Failing to understand someone, I tell myself that he's stupid; but when I fail to understand a second person, I'm afraid it's the world that I don't understand

Silently to a woman seen from behind: "The Lord help you if you're not beautiful!"

I broke an apple in two with my hands, and at first it gave off a disgusting smell, as though in protest against my violence

The poodle stands in the open shop door, looking proud enough to be the owner

"Perception is attention" (Novalis): an attention that emanates from the perceptible object; my wish to go out into the street as a wish to experiment ("Don't look for anything behind phenomena; they themselves are the doctrine"—Goethe)

"Do you still think of me sometimes?" — "Yes, when masturbating. Afterwards I forget you instantly"

Between houses in the distance, a sudden flight of pigeons: rock splinters thrown up by an explosion

The moment in the day when I lose control

Finding an experience described offers the possibility of experiencing something similar that has never been described (nothing has ever been described)

A resolute glare

Surrounded by screaming children: build up strength

Midnight. Far down the street, people slinking past like stray dogs

A silly, "humorous" day: house full of visitors

"Call up sometime when you're feeling rotten." — "Pardon me, but I never listen to such remarks"

My way of thinking: for a while I think freely and aimlessly, letting my thoughts take care of themselves, so to speak; then I stop and rethink everything I've thought during that first interval; then I rethink what I've rethought, etc.; then once more I give myself over to the confusion of my thoughts, fantasies, memories, wishes, obsessions, until the next arbitrary stop; what has been several times rethought then serves as material for further free and aimless thinking, etc.

In the presence of adult strangers, I often, in sheer embarrassment, look at the children

Although I express myself far more than I used to by mere gestures or facial expressions, I believe I'm still too voluble; instead of talking too much, I mug and gesticulate too much

The sleeping child's hands smell of chocolate

Deserted street at night; at last it shows perspective

Just before falling asleep, I like to let my ghosts out and walk them, so to speak, like dogs (but tonight they wouldn't budge)

Silly phrase: "He is incapable of enjoyment." I am convinced that everyone is capable of enjoyment

Wild desire to shoot an arrow into the fire

Time spent with most people seems to me as devoid of feeling, as destructive of feeling, as office time

G. says: "That's beautiful," even before it becomes beautiful

Night, sky, stars, fences give an impression of hypocrisy under the full moon: they pretend to know nothing of death; a clear moonlit night is so disgustingly upper-crust

February

A. points to a brand of chocolate: "Why isn't it ever advertised? I never see it in the commercials"

A ski jumper lost his balance in mid-air. The camera followed him a long way as he twisted and turned and tried to maneuver himself into a non-fatal position. Then he disappeared out of the picture and he hasn't been found to this day

Loveless day. And the night resounds with the signals of the railroad workers

Because of this stupid person beside me, my attentiveness strikes me as affected and I feel that I, too, am getting stupid; at the same time, I feel responsible for the other person's stupidity. Result: stupid politeness, polite stupidity

At the *crémerie*: for the moment, the women are alone with their tubs of butter

Yesterday, heavy backwash of the past, hopeless lethargy: all afternoon I lay there, incapable of moving, wishing there were some way of moving myself by remote control; little by little, by thinking and by calling forth images for the state I was in, I rebuilt my person from the hideous nothing I had become (a hostile, ice-covered land mass, my chest encumbered with a windowless fortress in which a prisoner was making a speech consisting of unconnected words)

Sometimes at least I am able to summon up the dignity of a failure

My mother came toward me on the hilltop; she was with someone else. From a distance her face was friendly and healthy. When we met, I asked her if she was at last dead. She said yes; her face, which had seemed friendly from far off, had now become the smooth face of an avenger. "Why," I screamed, "must you dead people all have such frozen faces?" She looked at me unmoved, her face only became colder than ever

Narcissism in mid-winter

Briefly the strength to endure indifference; an inspired sort of indifference (toward myself)

He thought until language "became effective," until a new language came into being; this at last he called thinking

Merciless children

Organ music: this music, it seems to me, must have a source; it cannot have come into existence by and for itself; it arouses the thought of a higher being, something I cannot conceive of in any other context

Good writer: language aware of itself; great writer: transcending self-awareness, language opens up to something other than itself

My favorite company: the sleeping child

As we were passing a parked car today, someone stuck his head out the window. It flashed through my mind that if he were to point a gun at me I wouldn't push A. away but hold her in front of me (cowardice reflex)

Evening rush hour in the Métro. We stare at each other without pity; even at children we all stare without pity

Fantasy in a crowd: all these heads are cages; many different thoughts, but all equally captive; clipped thoughts in cages

Someone on the phone: "Come quickly!" — "Why?" — "I'm so beautiful right now"

Gradually learning to *think* about social questions

At last two enemies find the saving *phrase* that makes agreement possible

What do I want? What is real to me? (Two essential questions for my writing)

The patience of cowardice (but not the cowardice of patience)

Recovered my consciousness of self; now I can look at myself again

I *resolved* to sleep without worry; and I succeeded

Waking from the vertical plane of dreams to the diffuse horizontal plane of newspapers and daily affairs; in my dreams I had done nothing but wrong, now I am restored to a provisional rightness

Once again an almost wishful war fantasy: as if a war were needed to open up the outside world, to strip off the dead skin—and in the morning a strong anti-war feeling at the sight of a little tea strainer, as though this were a weapon against war, invented by a true man of peace (then suddenly all the little objects charged with peace energies flare up around me)

Fear sickens me, because only a part of me knows fear, while the rest of me doesn't believe in it (and is opposed to it); in the end the two parts clash, and that's where sickness comes in

As I was waking up, one of the objects moved, and it was me; I was a crater, and at the edge of this crater I was able with great difficulty to distinguish a few others (in waking I had felt myself to be a shell crater in a landscape of objects)

On a talk show: someone questions a panel of historians about the private life of a certain historical personage: a smile passes from one to the other; then they answer with forbearance

Progress in art: to get along without horror

The friendliness of the meat grinder at the supermarket to-day: one among many indications of people's courage; sweet, defiant little barriers to death; gadgets for carrying on

Maxim: Lock your opinions tight inside you, until they vanish

"Talk" has been so defamed that, however serious, however excellent, hardly anyone takes it seriously any more

I said enthusiastically to A.: "And tomorrow we'll stay home!" —just as I might formerly have announced an adventure or a trip

How often I am prevented by "what people think" from thinking in freedom

"Too stupid to be alone"

Sudden suspicion: that if I went mad I would only make a fool of myself; that I'd be an idiotic madman

The more rejected, hopeless, confused he felt when alone, the prouder and more self-assured he was in his public appearances

I'm able to think of her only when I reproach myself for my failings toward her; then she takes shape for me—when I simply want to think of her, she stays away

Never again will I try to "mean something" to a woman; horrified at the thought of a woman saying I had been important to her, that she had learned from me

Growing older, stronger through bursts of silence

What an effort it costs me to accept help! (If ever I've asked for help, it has been in such a feeble voice that only refusal was thinkable)

Tiredness—the water level drops and the objects on the river-bed are uncovered, sheet metal with sharp rusty edges

My teeth were clenched on opinions, but the sight of a girl on an escalator relaxed me, set me free; she looked at me as if she needed me, at least for the time it took her to ride past

After reading some stupid nonsense, I felt like looking at a map

Insensible with fatigue, I keep making mechanical attempts at sympathy; like wanting to help someone in a dream and not being able to

Wish-fantasy of a state of happiness, which would also make me practical

N. and I are almost always embarrassed when together, but we have come to take this pleasantly for granted ("pleasantly for granted")

Disgruntled: as if I'd become too small for my mold (like a shrunken, dried-out pudding)

The hostility of one enlightened woman to another: she never says anything bad about her, never speaks of disliking her—instead, she complains that the other woman dislikes *her* (new kind of enmity, where solidarity is usual)

I prepare myself for the hug, but also for the embarrassment after it

That ideal being, the "great actor," has been on my mind again: a complete man would, by definition, have to be a great actor as well

When in the course of a day speech is generated, rises to consciousness, is discovered: animation of dead nature

Pain in the legs from dissembling

The man caressed the back of his wife's hand by pushing the skin away from him

And once again, no doubt—I thought gloomily—I'll end by growing fond of these total strangers (and so I did)

Sitting by the sea, though I don't need it

The repulsive thing about strangers: I haven't yet recognized their faults and misdeeds as my own

"It does not strike me as impossible that a really adequate record of the thoughts of a whole lifetime, though seemingly without unity, might produce a shattering artistic effect. Yet this is a physical impossibility, it cannot be seriously attempted. But one can think of such possibilities, and strive for effects that came as close to them as is in our power" (Robert Musil, *Diaries*)

The woman with the Siamese cat and the photographs of cats all over her apartment; in conversation, she takes on the sudden, artificial, grimacing smile—it seizes hold of her whole face—which some people show when talking to animals or small children, and which is first recognizable by a crinkling of the nose, around which it builds up (cold, cold world)

Something to steer clear of: "writing as an instrument of revenge"; I will never be capable of that kind of writing

Moving down corridors with as little dignity as any other hotel guest

On top of the wall, against the sky, a plant with a white feather caught in it; behind it, the sky and its feathery clouds

Saw a performance of one of my plays: learned to bear guilt feelings with equanimity

Trembling old women who pass me in the street—how often I've thought that this was their last stroll before taking to their deathbeds

I have the feeling that people who "just know me" but have no idea what I've done thus far in my life respect me more than those who "know all about me" and keep protesting their enthusiasm, but seem to think that I am under some obligation to prove myself in their eyes; there's not a spark of affection or even of insight in their "enthusiasm"

"So happiness did exist. Chwostik knew it by his own experience" (Doderer, *The Waterfalls of Slunj*)

The energy I need each day to idealize ruins that used to be people

Instead of developing the justified accusation, I kept bringing up new ones, more and more of which were unwarranted, until I had put myself in the wrong

It was only after offending him that I realized how lonely he was

Swarming with thoughts of murder as I lie here this afternoon without anger or will—in much the same way as hunger crops up, and one suddenly starts eating; afraid of being driven under remote control to kill the child; tried to fall asleep; the impulse to murder welled up like a joyless but irresistible vice

In a world of luxury there would be no sounds (and no sucking on pipes)

The only tolerable stance for people with cameras: running —running fast

Sign of a great writer (Doderer): from him one accepts practical advice for everyday life

If I didn't write, I would hurt other people even more

Disgust: time and again it starts me thinking and stops me almost at once

Look at something until it gives my imagination a jolt

"A man who has worked with a scientific terminology for any length of time becomes speechless in his communication with himself: he can no longer make himself understood and is no longer understood by his own 'I'; the 'I' cannot be addressed in such terms" (Doderer, *The Waterfalls of Slunj*)

I have not been able to rediscover myself, because I was never lost; that, too, is a kind of loss

I slept until, still sleeping, I felt that I was missing something

Every taste I have not savored to the full seems to come back as a bad taste

Sometimes in forced conversations with a stranger I get the feeling that one of us, as the talk becomes more and more frantic and intense, will suddenly give up and run away screaming or sock the other in the jaw

When I accuse myself, I cannot contradict; but if it were only someone else reproving me—I could refute him at once and show him that I'm the better man

Periods of dullness in the course of the day—but then when I retrace my thoughts I see that I have been circling around essentials the whole time—but without passion, without excitement, without enlisting body and soul, just letting my thought pass by, but never letting it become a thought-action, no-sooner-thought-than-done—and that was what gave me my feeling of hopeless dullness

In my ignorance and idiocy, I looked into the radiant blue sky and suddenly understood how someone could become the founder of a religion (nothing much else for me to become)

Passing fantasy that Central Europe is the "original scene," and that its houses, streets, television sets, etc.—but not those to be found elsewhere—are also originals

In childhood, my love expressed itself as fear

When this woman's lover speaks to her, she follows his lip movements with her head

In anger the child lowers her eyelashes *monumentally*

Motive for suicide: people respected him too much

Today I haven't thought anything through—left alone, I watched the sky drifting away; fantasy that my head is flat after a day of thoughtlessness and listening to the news

With the insensibility of a long sleeper

The one thing that really counts: wavering glances

March

At least I've progressed to the point where no one can feel sorry for me

Success: I looked lovingly at the beautiful disorder on the table and managed to disregard the dirt on the floor

I cannot be serene unless I am doing some duty (to me, serenity is an active state)

The stillness of spring; white clouds in the morning sky; the barking of dogs like a whiplash

Watching television, I feel that I'm neglecting thought—and in the next moment it occurs to me that thoughts, or "thought" as such, are old hat by comparison with television, a futile illusion of past glory

A child who decides not to be afraid of school any more (bored with her own fear)

I glance at my notebooks and a feeling of confidence comes over me, starting from inside, from the middle of my chest; I feel strong, but only because something gentle is going on inside me (my personal epic, I thought)

Actually, I had no more illusions than he did, but to differentiate myself from him I played the lover of life and the world. It wasn't long before he came out with cheerful opinions, wishes, etc., and at that point I wanted to be cynical again

Inwardly I expressed my sympathy in complete sentences ("I feel sorry for her," etc.)—an indication that I didn't feel any pity, but only wanted to (once I had made that clear to myself, I was so pleased that I could have been nice to anybody)

Trying to devise a system of Taylorism for my inner and outward movements, a way of achieving maximum results with the least possible motion, in the kitchen, for instance (the minimum of gesture, by which I recognize great actors), as though that would give me strength and self-confidence—but I find that when *I* attempt such a system, the result is not the "charm of a great actor" but the clumsy, schematic movements of Frankenstein's monster

The height of the ridiculous: emerging freshly shorn from the barbershop

She dreamed with clenched fists, as though fighting back pain

A man came toward me with a Great Dane and I reached for my notebook as for a weapon

I must get over my "first glance" opinions, which are always deluding me and which are the source of all contempt and hate; almost inclined to think that generalized hate, to the point of war, springs from reliance on first glances (at second glance, it goes without saying, people will all love each other, etc.: the absurdity of the second glance, how sanctimonious and dismally unalterable it is)

In love with other people's melancholy

Concretizing the phrase "beside himself with anger": descending a flight of stairs in my rage, I suddenly felt like a

Moses figure, no longer my living, breathing self, but literally "beside myself"

Certain places in the modern world seem to exist only as garbage, no longer possible to use, enter, or even perceive; for instance, cafés with pinball machines, snack bars, waiting rooms, youth hostels, freeways, airports . . . and the people in such places no longer seem to exist; defying perception, they have ceased to be anything more than emptied tales (only the "Angel of Pinball Parlors" can save them)

The bounty of friendship after an undigested disappointment

On suffering injustice: I feel as if I had gigantic ears, enormous sore ears as *pars pro toto*

I notice that lately I've only been telling myself to be afraid, as if it were a kind of duty

"I shall create great art—for I have been wronged!"

The beautiful woman on the train: instead of staring at her, I should use my energy trying not to forget her

So inexperienced at showing my feelings that, real as they are, I have to act them out; a paradoxical deception, the simulation of genuine feelings; even such dissembling can be comforting

On all sides the waters rose, silently, inexorably: my body was washed away, and I found myself in a land of primeval rivers, thousands of years ago. An Assyrian army blocked my way. I was wearing a sweater, and that saved me from being pierced by a javelin. I had become a Jew. A taxi driver gave me a lift to Damascus. I wanted to have my hair cut and my beard shaved off right away. I saw myself in the dark stagnant water of an artificial pond, into which at nightfall the news was to be poured by way of a sluice. But no news came. My structure (my solid body, which I had acquired by thought and work in the last few years) failed to come back—and even now that I'm awake, everything is still gone, still washed away; all-embracing grief; but also a sense of dignity

The most terrible people: those who manage to make one feel guilty for states they have induced in themselves

The red can of shaving cream: intense experience of an object through memory of a toy car the same color, thirty years ago, on the footpath of a broad avenue of trees: a purely abstract object which gave me a feeling of triumph: freshness, newness, splendor (with the rubble of war in the background)

Stroboscopic effect of fear

People incapable of imagination, who look at all others with an evil eye

The wrong gestures I make in the course of the day: I need them precisely because they have turned out to be wrong; without them I'd be lost

"Withdrawal of love"! There's no such thing; if love is there, how can anyone withdraw it?

"I am harmonious by nature: as a child I was often caressed in my sleep"

Adult-imposed order must be a source of suffering to a child who has not yet acquired a sense of order

Dejection: slow-moving dreams; and nothing happens—no plot

If a child is wakened every morning with music, even of the gentlest, most comforting sort—doesn't it seem likely that he'll end up hating all music?

Why not make pets of things (the sweater and socks, for instance, that are drying on the radiator) to welcome me back affectionately after a hard night?

I smirked as if I had been responsible for the perfect moment, which had happened by pure chance

In the dusk the new green in the garden startles one with a light of its own

The barber stands in the doorway and watches his passing victims

My sincerity was undiminished, but after a few hours I felt it had become an act and that I could only keep it up by acting

D. told me about a woman and her child: the angrier the woman got, the more softly she spoke to the child; not the slightest gesture, she just spoke more and more softly; and D. remembered that when she herself was little and her mother had scolded her, she could always tell by the movements of her mother's hands that she was sorry to have to scold, that the things she was obliged to say made her miserable; this knowledge had been a comfort to D. By contrast, this woman's utter immobility when angrily imploring her child (she wasn't well, she had begged her time and time again to spare her nerves); what a hard time this child would have with her mother, D. thought, if anything really serious should happen

Today, on a certain occasion, I actually succeeded in having no opinion (experience of activity)

I left the people I was with as though emerging from a long interrogation in which no confession had been wrung from me

The most mindless of mortals: those who only leaf through books

With one hand I manipulated objects; I kept the other in readiness to comfort them if necessary

This evening all the individual sounds I hear fuse into music in my mind

All the time I was talking to this man, I saw how impatient he was to interrupt me; but when I stopped talking, he didn't say a word; after that, he was just a listener

Most people seem unable to emerge from themselves without a dialogue written expressly for them

Bresson: the beautiful and never-changing humorlessness of amateur actors—their total commitment (they never smile during or after their speeches, as professional actors often do)

The businesswoman: when her voice is not operating at the speed of a machine, she becomes terrifyingly understanding and seductive

So many years of freedom: why wouldn't I have an inspired moment now and then?

He looked severely at the landscape, like an artisan looking around him before starting on an important job, to make sure all his tools are in the right place

"With the disappearance of supernatural life in man, his natural life becomes guilt, but that does not deter him from offending against morality" (Benjamin on *The Elective Affinities*)

While glancing through my notebooks: a sense of time earned and gained ("What will you be able to write about after this?" — "About snow in the Rocky Mountains")

Think away the naturalistic forms until didactic, demonstrative forms (Brecht) result; think away the didactic forms until mythical forms result (my writing)

Someone arrives from a foreign country on a plane that is very late. A few steps away from the place where he has an appointment, he starts to run

I managed, in her presence, to lose myself in thought; when I emerged, I involuntarily called her by the wrong name

While still awake, I laughed about a dream I was already having

No poem possible without an acute need

I noticed that something I intended to say was stupid; then I said it all the same, as though under compulsion, and once spoken, it became even stupider; but at least I had done a kind of duty

Thoughts while looking at most people: they've never read a word about the way they stand there, the way they walk, etc.; they've never read anything at all—if they had, they'd be different (What stops me from denouncing these people, and in the strongest, most virulent terms?)

I often feel that I am my own employee

When as a child I first experienced *myself* as a ghostly event in the symbol-free everyday world, I knew that my self would keep me busy for the rest of my life (that I would never finish thinking myself through)

While listening to someone, I felt in my eyes an attentiveness without strain—and I did not, as sometimes happens, feel forced to ponder a possible answer while the other was still talking

I shouted something at A. from a distance; hearing me, she took on a stilted, artificial attitude, which was supposed to indicate interest but produced an effect of arrogance and indifference; it was only when I came closer and repeated what I had said that she unbent, shook off her artificial atti-tude, and became a child again, just listening (being spoken to from a distance had sparked off her reflex—the haughty pose of a grownup woman)

The man outside the station tried to kiss the woman goodbye, and the woman, who had apparently been on intimate terms with him only recently, resisted stubbornly: their strangely regular movements suggested a new kind of dance, more beautiful than any formal dance, more alive—and I looked on as a dance was born, as it were, from an episode of everyday life

The full moon in the morning over the rooftops, which are already shimmering green in the rising sunlight: to me this morning full moon has the look of a real planet with continents, almost identical with the earth; similar people in similar towns are just beginning their day, and there is regular plane service from here to there, as between all industrial countries; yes, the moon looks to me like an industrial country, and leaves me with a strangely comfortable feeling: how pleasant to be living in an industrial country with a likeness, a twin planet, that forms a disk in the sky

A tall crane, half immersed in shaving cream, toppled over after its sections had buckled one by one. I was the only eyewitness here in the house. Another catastrophe! I cried. We ran out into the courtyard; there lay the top of the crane, which had crushed the whole city under it. A man ran by, his body covered with shaving cream. A dead man's face came to light: his eyes and eyebrows were perfectly round in death

I stood on the station platform and as the people poured out of the train I searched for the familiar face; at the moment, all these strangers seemed more attractive than the known face I was waiting for

When the car refuses to start, the driver gives the steering wheel an offended look

A day of restless flights; then a surge of warmth: love

Over the years I've lost my connection with my writing hand (in my childhood there was a natural unity between me and the letters it formed)

A man and a woman locked in a long, motionless embrace. I wonder how they can stand it and what stops them from melting into each other; maybe this long-lasting, still embrace just isn't the real thing

Refrain from opinions and keep observing until at last the gravitational pull of a life-feeling sets in

Deep in my inwardness I warmed myself, beyond reach of the functional world

Mediocre music: I have to think up an idea to go with it; then I can like it

Moment of quiet friendliness: as though my eyes had broadened into a wide screen

Perfect charm, presence of mind, and freedom—all achieved by means of a well-conducted amorous "adventure" (but not a single false move or word, or the whole thing degenerates into bedroom comedy)

To an acquaintance of long standing who has finally become a friend: "Those were the days when I couldn't tell you anything"

Last night: so happy that I lost all sense of place. A feeling no longer of omnipotence but of oneness with the world

How quickly I forget that a certain person and I were tired together (tired in a way that creates a bond)

Argumentative drunk: "Am I right or am I wrong?" (The embarrassing solemnity of drunks)

My longing for inoffensive people, in whose company I, too, will pass for inoffensive

Perception, the incorporation of others into myself: at last I can defend myself

As though passion had charred my bones

A great actor like Robert De Niro speaks and moves like model and copy in one (he exists, and in existing describes a life); envious thought that with their intense, selfless concern for others such actors are the true writers: *their* writing is self-explanatory (like Henry Fonda's movements, which appear to me as letters)

By evening I had at last—once again—thought myself free: in that moment I raised my head

About the Author

Peter Handke was born in Griffen, Austria, in 1942. After graduating from a Catholic seminary in 1959 he studied law at the University of Graz. Handke first attracted public notice in 1966 when he delivered an unprecedented attack on contemporary German writing at a seminar at Princeton University. That same year saw the publication of his first novel, *The Hornets*, and his first stage success, *Offending the Audience*. With Wim Wenders, he wrote the screenplay for the critically acclaimed film *Wings of Desire*, released in 1988. His other works include *Repetition* (1988), *Across* (1986), *Slow Homecoming* (1985), *2 X Handke* (1977), and *3 X Handke* (1972), all of which are available from Collier Books. Peter Handke is widely regarded as the most important postmodern writer since Beckett. He lives in Salzburg, Austria.